AZOR'S REDEMPTION

David A. Talbot

Copyright © 2020 David A. Talbot
All rights reserved
First Edition

PAGE PUBLISHING, INC.
Conneaut Lake, PA

First originally published by Page Publishing 2020

ISBN 978-1-6624-0142-8 (pbk)
ISBN 978-1-6624-1501-2 (hc)
ISBN 978-1-6624-0143-5 (digital)

Printed in the United States of America

INTRODUCTION

"On Azcob's throne, I swear that it is important I get my personal property today," Alan Eliot said, pleading with the guard.

The prison guard's name was James Pike. He was average height, but overweight as most of the prison guards were. Pike didn't like his life or his job and, in turn, tried to make the prisoners he was in charge of, as miserable as his limited authority would allow.

"You know the rules, Eliot. You'll get your stuff after the property officer goes through it and sends it down to us."

Then, with a look of wonder on his face, Pike said, "What was it you said a minute ago? You swear on whose throne?"

"Never mind," Alan said, shaking his head. He then began pacing his empty cell with the look of a man carrying a tremendous weight on his shoulders.

Pike walked away from Alan's cell, thinking, *These prisoners always act like they have some major appointment to keep.* He laughed a hateful laugh that echoed throughout the cellblock as he slammed the steel gate shut.

Alan stopped his pacing and started doing pushups to occupy his mind and expel some of the anxious energy he felt coursing through him. Alan was a muscular, six-foot tall man with blond hair and blue eyes and was considered a good-looking twenty-six-year-old. His good-natured personality reflected his usual good moods. But today, Alan was in a very anxious mood because he didn't know how long it would be before he got his property back.

In that small number of belongings was a very old, dog-eared book that held the key to life or possible death for the world of Azor.

Every time Alan was moved to a different cellblock of the prison that he was serving time in, the property department would take his limited belongings and inventory them extensively. Each inmate was allowed only a restricted number of property, and depending on which block you were housed in, you were allowed specific items in your cell. Alan was moved often because of his past attempts to escape from the prison. Oftentimes, the property department would get his stuff to him in a day's time. In these instances, Alan would only miss one night without his book, but other times, it would take days or weeks to get his stuff returned to him, and he would miss many nights without his beloved book.

Alan stopped doing pushups and sat on his bunk, sweating profusely; he was trying not to think of the consequences if he didn't get his property back sooner. Every night that passed here was a day and a night in Azor, and when he last left Azor, the wicked wizard Krem was supposedly putting a peace treaty together to be delivered to Emperor Azcob. Alan just wasn't convinced of Krem's recent change of heart. Alan knew that until he got his book back, there was nothing he could do other than worry about what was taking place in his absence. He hoped sorceress Aztrion was healing from her accident and Azonia was safe. Oh, my beautiful Azonia.

Alan closed his eyes and conjured up a visual of Azonia in his mind—long shiny black hair that seemed to always move on its own, even when there wasn't even a whisper of a breeze. She was shorter than Alan by a foot, but she stood so straight and proud that you didn't notice her shortness. Her skin was the color of the milky earth moon on a clear night, and her gold eyes sparkled with the brilliance of a vault full of diamonds and rubies. Alan knew he loved her from the moment he first met her.

Sitting in his cell, with his breathing starting to return to normal from the many pushups, he decided worrying about the unknown in Azor was fruitless. He would occupy his mind with something else. Alan thought back on his life and what led to the day he found the book that enabled him to first travel to the land of Azor.

CHAPTER ONE

Alan Eliot was born in 1964 into a middle-class family. His father was a construction worker, who worked hard to support his family. Alan had one older sister and two younger brothers. His parents had a restless spot in their hearts, which is referred to as Gypsy blood. They moved about every six months, always looking for that perfect place to live, and it was always the next town in the next state.

By the time Alan was fourteen, he had lived in many states in the United States of America. When he was fourteen, he started to get into trouble with the law, as he had a desire for excitement. Breaking the law and taking the chance of getting caught provided him with the adrenaline shots he craved.

When the courts eventually wanted to lock him up, Alan knew he couldn't live long being caged. He needed his freedom, to explore and find new and exciting ways to quench his thirst for excitement and travel, which he inherited from his parents. Alan chose to run away from the law to keep what he so badly craved. So at fourteen, he escaped his court-ordered confinement and found himself on the run. He started out with a backpack and an atlas of the United States highways.

In the beginning, he traveled to places he had lived as a kid, hitchhiking from one place to the next. He looked up old friends and old neighborhoods, but at his age, he couldn't stay in one place very long without adults starting to question how a kid was out on his own. So Alan moved on. The more places he went and saw, the more he wanted to see. In a two-year period, Alan succeeded in hitchhiking to every state in the United States, except Alaska and Hawaii, only because there weren't any highways to take him there.

Alan's grandmother, Rose, insisted he call her weekly, so she would know he was safe. Rose wished he would tire of his traveling. She worried about him. Eventually, she realized it kept him happy, so she outfitted him with a top-notch backpack and sleeping bag.

Alan ran into dangers traveling the roads alone, but it only fed his desire for living on the edge. At times, he endured some tough periods of winter cold and hunger, but it was a small price to pay for his freedom. When Alan was almost seventeen, his grandma Rose told him of the death of his father. He had died of lung cancer. Alan came home for the first time in years to attend the funeral.

The loss of his father was tough on him; the man had lived only fifty-two years and died with so many dreams and goals set aside for the sake of his family. Alan actually felt guilt at being able to chase his dreams while his father no longer could. So he settled down with Grandma Rose for a while.

He took a job in a lumber yard to pay room and board.

Eventually, as always, the undeniable desire for excitement got him in trouble with the law. His disregard for the rules and his prior escape from justice landed him in jail for a term of fifteen years.

The structure of his particular sentence allowed for him to possibly receive parole for good behavior after eighteen months. At first, prison was a new experience, and it filled the void that he needed so badly to fulfill. But as time went on and the newness wore off, he felt like the walls were closing in on him more every day. He needed desperately to ramble. He found small doses of excitement by getting in trouble even though this jeopardized his chance for getting parole.

He felt trapped and stifled, counting the days till he could get out.

When his eighteenth month hearing arrived, he was denied parole, based on the trouble he had gotten into in order to receive that small, quick dose of excitement. He was told he could possibly get out at his next hearing in eight months but only if he behaved in the interim. The only solace was that he was going to be granted lower security housing for the eight-month period.

Alan was moved to the minimum-security prison a few weeks later and immediately found himself planning his escape. There was only one fence holding him back, and an uncontrollable urge drove him to get free from this cage, so within three days, he escaped. Alan headed for California riding a cloud weaved from the adrenaline of being free and on the run at the same time. Now this was more like it, a feeling he couldn't describe but loved every exhilarating moment of.

Four months passed. The freedom was like a breath of life for him. The extra boost of being a wanted man wore off in time, and he found himself testing the boundaries of the law again, just to feed the untamable desire for a dose of adrenaline. Of course, this behavior resulted in getting him arrested and then brought back to Massachusetts to face his sentence and a new escape charge.

More time and trouble went by slowly and painfully until Alan was paroled two years later. The rules of parole denied him the freedom of travel, so once again, he took flight, and it was only a matter of time before he was picked up on a parole warrant in Georgia and returned again to Massachusetts in 1991. The state determined Alan had been given his last opportunity to embarrass them, and as a result, he would serve the remainder of his sentence in a maximum-security prison. Alan's need for *freedom and excitement*, cost him those very same things, for many years to come.

Alan rebelled strongly against his self-inflicted punishment and got into even more trouble, resulting in him losing even the little freedom he had within the prison. He was restricted to his cell and felt he would shrivel and die, as a green plant will without water, air, and sun.

Alan eventually found that reading enabled him to get small doses of freedom and escape, as well as excitement. He had a special ability of becoming the character in the book, actually manifesting in his mind and heart what the author of the story so badly wanted the reader to experience in his or her writing. This was sufficient to keep Alan alive inside, and he read every book he could get his hands on. His favorites were fantasy and science fiction; they seemed most capable of stimulating his imagination and need for excitement. He would read until his body begged for sleep, then he would dream about what he read. Upon waking, he would read again, weeks and months flew by this way.

He had no responsibilities. His meals were brought to his cell, and he only left his cell for showers and short trips to the library. While on these short library trips, Alan searched the shelves one book at a time, looking for any science fiction or fantasy book he had not already read. The library wasn't well-maintained, and none of the books were in order or catalogued, so he spent most of his allotted time searching through the many books to find the ones he wanted and needed so badly.

Eventually the science fiction and fantasy books were harder and harder to find as he had read most of them. There came a day when he couldn't find even one. He knew he had only an hour to search, and as the time ticked away, his search became more frantic. He looked over at the clock, and only twenty minutes remained before he would be forced to return to his cell.

"There has to be one. Be calm. Take your time, and you'll find one," he said quietly to himself.

Before he knew it, the guard yelled, "Five minutes left, Eliot!"

Alan started darting from shelf to shelf, looking and looking, the voice in his head repeating, "I have to find one! I have to!"

He knocked over a whole row of books that landed on the floor with a dull smack. As he bent to pick them up, the guard yelled, "What are you doing over there? If you rip any of those books, you'll pay for them! Let's go. Your time is up anyways."

In his head, Alan screamed, "*No! I have to find a book. Don't you understand? I must find something to read to get me through the week!*" But out loud, he said nothing. He knew he would lose his hour next week, so he quietly followed the guard back to his cell.

Back in his cell, he began pacing back and forth like a caged animal, not unlike the tigers do at the zoo.

"How am I going to make it a week?" he asked himself.

That week proved to be the hardest week of his nine years in prison to date. He tried to read a few books he had already read, but the excitement of a new adventure just wasn't there. If Alan had ever come close to just giving up, it was in that very long week. He attempted to work out to occupy the time, but there is only so much you can do in an empty six by eight.

Finally, the week passed, and it was time for Alan's hour in the library. With a feeling of dread, he checked the shelves closest to the guard's desk for possible books that had been returned by other prisoners during the week. Alan knew that the guard was lazy and returned books would be put on the closest shelves to his desk, so he wouldn't have to exert himself unnecessarily. When his search turned up no new science fiction or fantasy books, his anxiety level increased.

Alan gave thought to a series of science fiction books he had found way in the back of the library months earlier. They were written in the 1940s and were a very good read, about life on Mars.

"Why hadn't I thought to look back there again?" Alan questioned of himself out loud.

He walked quickly to the back's corner shelf and searched for the series on Mars. It was there, right where he had replaced it. Alan always made sure he replaced the books back where he had found them prior to reading them. He did this in case other prisoners also went through the books systematically as he did.

Alan's hopes grew as he thumbed through the eleven-book series on Mars. He thought back to how he enjoyed the story of John Carter of Earth, who had gone to Mars and experienced one adventure after another.

Alan checked the rest of the books on the shelf containing the Mars series, but no other science fiction or fantasy books were to be found there. Upon further searching, he realized that the whole six rows of shelves in that section were all very old books. All the books in the section had the initials R. W. on the top part of the binding, as if they were from someone's personal collection.

This realization brought encouragement and energy to his search, as it stood to reason that anyone who owned and read the Mars series, was sure to have delved deeper into that genre of writing. With renewed hope, he began searching the other shelves more closely. On the third shelf, he came across a book with a note taped to the cover. The tape was old and yellowed, as was the paper the note was written on, and it came loose in his hand as he touched it. The note was difficult to clearly make out, but Alan read slowly.

To: Walpole Prison Library

From: Joyce West

Dear prison officials,

My father, Richard West, has been a missing person for the past eight years. Our family has finally come to the realization he will not be returning and has thus declared him deceased. We are in the process of settling his estate and have come to a decision to donate his book collection to the prison library.

Sincerely,

The estate of Mr. Richard West

Reading this note sent Alan's imagination into a tailspin of different scenarios to explain Mr. West's disappearance.
"Maybe aliens came down from space and abducted him for testing. Maybe he built a time machine and went into the past and a computer chip burned out, stranding him there."
Alan drifted back to reality, realizing he only had a half hour left in the library. He attacked the remaining two shelves with a feeling of reserved confidence.
While going through the books on the second-to-last shelf, he found a very old leather-bound, dog-eared book. He could tell this book had been read so much that the title was worn right off the soft leather cover. He opened it to the first page but found it blank—no author, no publishing company, and no copyright date or information. This was unusual. He flipped to the next page where there was a short poem in the middle of the page.

> Of freedom, true love, and peace I have dreamed,
> Never in my wildest imaginings could I have seen,
> A world as beautiful as Azor.
> So read at night and not before,
> And if you believe, really believe,
> You too may find the door.

Alan's heart skipped a beat. He was sure this was a science fiction or fantasy book. He quickly flipped through the pages and found there to be twenty-five chapters, each about a page long.

Alan's hour was up, he closed the beautiful, old leather book and put it under his arm and walked back to his cell with a smile on his face.

As the guard was locking him in, he said, "You look better than you did last week. Prison must agree with you!" He laughed sadistically as he walked away.

It didn't bother Alan; he was too busy with his own thoughts. He sat on his bunk running his hand over the smooth cover of the book with no title.

Alan spoke softly to the book, "I will wait until dark to read you as the poem says."

CHAPTER TWO

Alan had only about three hours to go until sunset. He decided that it must be considered night at sunset. He reread the poem again, and it said simply *night*, no specific time. Sunset was at about 7:00 p.m. this time of year, and it was only 5:00 p.m. now, two hours to go.

The guard had just finished bringing around the evening meal. It was cold as usual and quite slimy-looking also. It consisted of two processed turkey slices, fake mashed potatoes, frozen sliced carrots, and colored water, referred to as "bug juice." For desert, they served two small chocolate chip cookies, which were so hard they would cut your gums if you didn't dip them in the bug juice first.

Alan was excited but anxious about reading the book. He really didn't feel much like eating, but he ate the whole meal anyways, mainly to take up some time. After eating, he washed up and brushed his teeth; he even shaved just to pass the time. It was now only 5:30 p.m. The more time that passed, it seemed the slower time went. Alan picked up the book once again and rubbed his fingers across the worn cover.

"How old are you? What happened to Mr. West? If only you could talk, you could tell me about all your owners, where you came from, why no copyright. I am sure that's a story in itself," said Alan.

He laid the book down on the table, then lay on his bunk with his hands folded behind his head.

He stared at the book on his table, saying, "What adventure do you hold for me? What is this world of Azor? Another planet, an alternate universe perhaps? A fantasyland?"

He thought, *I must be crazy, talking to a book. I have read thousands of books. What makes this one so special?*

Alan knew before he even asked that question, that this was no ordinary book. He sat up and reached out, picking up the book again. His inspection determined that even as dog-eared and worn as it was, he was sure he had never seen such a handsome book. It was in that moment he decided that this was one book he wouldn't be returning to the library. He would keep it as his own. He was sure that if Mr. West were here today, he would want it kept by someone who could truly appreciate its beauty.

It was now 6:45 p.m., only twenty minutes to go.

"What to do for twenty minutes?"

Alan decided that exercise would best take up the remaining time. He had a deep respect for martial arts. He practiced and did his stretching routine often. This was a perfect time for the relaxed feeling he received from practicing the arts. He stretched his legs, taking about five minutes; then his back, another five minutes. Still, there were ten minutes to go. He went through his blocks and strike regiments, which took him right up to 7:05 p.m. He was winded, but in good enough shape that he immediately settled down. He sat on his bunk and looked at the book lying on his desk. He reached out for it for the third time, this time knowing he would get to read it. He fluffed up his pillow and lay back on his bunk to read.

Just as he was going to open the book, he said, "What if it isn't as good as I have led myself to believe? Oh well, what the heck. Here we go."

Alan turned to the page with the poem he had read earlier and reread the last line.

"If you believe, really believe, you, too, may find the door."

Then he sighed, "Well, I waited till night as the poem said, I may as well follow instructions and believe."

He knew with his ability to become the person in a storyline and his vivid imagination, it would be easy for him to believe. Actually, he had believed for years that science fiction and fantasy books were based on truth in part. He also believed if people were able to get out of their own way, they could accomplish great feats. It is man's doubt that holds him back from using the majority of his brain. If only man didn't have years of deep-seated doubt, he could talk telepathically and move and shape things with his thoughts alone. Alan believed that *gifted* only meant "those that were able to tap into different sections of their brains." He was sure that magic powers were also hidden in that treasure trove of untapped knowledge—if only you could get by the doubt and just simply believe.

Alan turned to the first page and was shocked to see there weren't chapters but entries, as in a diary.

He read on.

Entry 1

Welcome to Azor. My name is Azterl. I am a wizard of the highest order on Azor. It is my honor to meet you based on your ability to even read what is written on these pages. The fact that you are able to read this, proves you have followed my instructions in the poem. If you had not read this at night and believed, then the words you are now reading would appear foreign to you and unreadable. Only a true believer reading this would invoke the spell that I placed on this book. Yet the spell placed on the poem would allow anyone in any world, land, or time to see the writing in their tongue. When I wrote it and sent it on its way, I had no way of telling where it would end up. Under normal circumstances, I would be able to trace the book with my magic, but the drain this spell will cause will most definitely kill me. My death is a small price to pay to ensure my beloved homeland of Azor is not locked in slavery. This would cause its destruction and absolute death. The world of Azor exists on its inhabitants' dreams and freedoms. There is so much I would like to tell you about my world, but time is running out. I must make many more entries in this book before sending it away and then pray for help to come.

Each of these entries will change, starting at entry number 2. The entries will pertain to your travels, so read each one carefully. The information will help you on your journey, which will take place at the end of each entry reading.

Keep in mind that this is a new experience. Stay alert, and when you see an opportunity, take advantage of it. Also, things may not always be as you see them.

Once again, be careful. I don't know where you are from, but the differences in our two worlds could be extreme. My time is running out for this entry, so I wish you a good and safe journey!

Repeat these words aloud, "In the name of wizard Azterl, I invoke his death spell."

Alan felt himself pulled into a void. He looked around and realized he was actually falling and moving sideways at the same time. There was nothing around or below him except utter darkness. He shut his eyes so tight that they hurt. He knew he was screaming but heard no sound.

Suddenly, he was aware that he was lying on his back once again on a hard surface. He dared not open his eyes right away. He just lay there, taking deep breaths in an attempt to calm the feelings of nausea.

Finally, he opened his eyes. The first thing he saw was a yellow sky with green clouds moving across it at a rapid rate. He rolled over and vomited in the purple grass he now realized he was lying on. He sat up and tried to orient himself, saying, "What is this? I must have drifted off to sleep while reading. This must be a dream! What if it isn't a dream and I am really on Azor?"

He laughed out loud, thinking of what the guard's face would look like when he made his count, and he was gone from his cell.

He was quickly brought back to the present as he stood up and looked around. He was standing in the middle of a purple meadow, surrounded on all sides by trees or what appeared to be trees. There was such a brilliant glare emanating from the base of the forest surrounding him that he couldn't look directly into it. He raised his eyes to look at the tops of the trees. The foliage was as purple as the meadow grass. Then Alan realized the sun was just rising, or what was the equivalent of earth's sun. This sun was a perfect square, with four different sections, each a different color he had never seen before. It was so beautiful, but his eyes began hurting from looking at it too long. It wasn't the brightness that caused the pain to his eyes but the strange, unfamiliar colors. Then he noticed that there was no breeze at all, even though the green clouds were moving across the yellow sky at such a high rate of speed. He noticed that he felt neither heat nor cold; he was simply comfortable.

"Imagine, a world with a perfect temperature!" he said aloud.

His own voice startled him because until now, he hadn't noticed it was perfectly quiet—no birds singing, no crickets or grasshoppers, no sound at all. Alan started walking toward the forest, in the direction the clouds were moving in, for lack of a better choice. He figured it would at least give him some type of compass.

As he approached the forest, he was better able to see the base of the trees more clearly. The trees were actually gold in color, which accounted for the glare coming from them. As he reached the edge of the forest and was standing right next to one of the trees, it appeared as if it was not only gold in color but real gold. He reached out and touched the surface, finding it smooth and cool to the touch. He pressed one of his fingernails into the tree and was able to leave a scratch mark behind.

"Gold? It is real gold! Now I know I am dreaming." He laughed louder than he meant to.

Alan moved on slowly through the quiet forest for quite some time.

After some more time, he thought to himself, *This is ridiculous! I am walking through a forest full of gold trees, on this world called Azor, and it seems like it's been hours now. I am tired of this forest. I am thirsty, and I am starting to get hungry as well. I wonder if I will just die in this forest of hunger and thirst before I even find anything or anyone. Wizard Azterl spoke of death and destruction in his first entry. How long ago was that? This world doesn't look destructed, but maybe everyone died long ago. I just have no way of knowing how long ago he wrote the book, or if anyone besides myself was able to read it. Maybe all the previous readers didn't believe and no help ever came to Azor. Now, here I am, a thousand, maybe a million years too late.*

All these thoughts depressed Alan, so he wiped them from his mind.

He thought he heard a sound, so he stopped and listened intently, but there was nothing. He had thought he heard the jingle of a small bell.

"It must be this total silence playing tricks on me," he said.

Just then, he heard it again. He cupped his hand to his ear to enable him to hear better. He was sure he heard bells. The bells sounded far off, but in the direction that he was headed. He walked on slowly and cautiously.

As he walked, he imagined all kinds of things.

Maybe its fairy or elf children wearing bells so that their parents could find them if they wandered too far from home. Maybe it is a horse's harness that got stuck around a dragon's neck while he was eating the horse.

That thought made Alan break out in a sweat regardless of the perfect temperature. He cleared that thought from his head, but he did proceed a little more cautiously. Alan froze as he heard a loud sound. The sound was not unlike the bleat of a lamb, but ten times as loud. The thought of the dragon popped back into his head. He shivered, and the hair stood up on the back of his neck. He moved forward and came to a clearing and stood just inside the tree line. The clearing wasn't very big, maybe one hundred yards in all. What he saw in the clearing scared him more than any nightmare ever could. He noticed there was a pool of water in the clearing. It was milky white, but it appeared to be water just the same. Regardless of the danger and fear he felt while looking at what surrounded the pool, he knew he would have to quench his thirst.

CHAPTER THREE

Alan made sure he was well-hidden behind the tree. He looked up at the sun and saw it was directly overhead. He figured if time ran the same as on earth, it should be about noon. He decided to sit and wait. Maybe they were just having lunch and then moving on. The *they* were three riding animals, but the weirdness of them is what first scared him. These creatures were the size of a rhinoceros but the similarities ended there. They had long black hair and six legs that ended in three-toed birdlike feet. They had no tails that he could see. Coming out of the head, where the eyes should have been, were two antennas about a foot long each. On top of these antenna were eyeballs, enabling the creature to see in any direction they wished, and maybe even more than one, as far as Alan could tell. The eyeballs seemed to move continuously, keeping a constant vigil of their surroundings, even as they dropped their heads to eat from the meadow grass.

The creatures wore a harness and a saddle-type seat that was more like a bed than a seat. As the creatures moved around the pool area, the harness and saddle made the bell sounds he had heard from deeper in the forest. He assumed that the loud bleating sound had come from these animals as well.

Sitting around the pool were three men. They were different from normal men, but still men just the same. They had long black hair that reached to their waists and stood about five feet tall. They had pale white skin, like chalk. They were eating something that appeared to be fruit the size of a melon. They ate the peel only and threw the inside portion to the riding beasts. The beasts quickly wolfed them down and patiently waited for more. The men seemed normal enough and didn't seem to have any weapons he could see.

"I'll just walk out and get some of that water, and maybe, they will share some of that fruit also."

Alan was just about to step out into the open when he noticed something he hadn't seen before. There was another person sitting on the ground about fifteen yards behind where the others were seated. One of the riding beasts had been blocking the person from his view earlier. As Alan took a harder look, he could tell now that it was actually a girl about twenty years old. She was chalk white, as the men were, except she had very long silver hair. Alan saw that she was bound to a golden post that was driven into the purple grass of the clearing. The girl's arms had been pulled back and tied behind the post. There was also a cloth rag tied around her mouth and head, as a gag. What bothered Alan most was that she seemed to be looking directly at him where he hid. He backed into the woods slowly and quietly, as not to attract the attention of the men or riding beasts. When he was well-covered by the forest again, he moved to his left about thirty yards. He then slowly moved out to the edge of the trees again and peered out at the group by the water. The men hadn't moved, but as he looked over in the girl's direction, she was once again staring right at him. He was sure she was aware of him now. She seemed to be staring at him pleadingly.

Alan wasn't sure what he should do, and he thought, *This isn't my world. Maybe this behavior is normal here, and I would be wrong to interfere. Wizard Azterl did say in his entry that the differences in our two worlds may be extreme. Should I just move on and make my first contact with the natives of this world, one of less controversy? But what if she is a prisoner? Didn't he also say that the world of Azor existed on its inhabitant's dreams and freedoms? I wish he had been clearer on his bits of supposed helpful information. I feel more confused and torn than helped. I suppose I can let the girl guide my decision.*

Alan looked up at the girl to be sure he had her attention still. She was looking right at him. Using his hands, he tried to get his point across to her. First, he pointed at himself, then at her, and then he made a running motion with his fingers. At first, Alan didn't think she understood until she looked over at the men to make sure they weren't paying attention. She moved her neck and head forward so her head indicated toward him and then dropped her chin down to her chest and moved her legs in a running motion. She seemed to take special care not to attract her captors' attention while doing this. Well, that seemed to be enough evidence for Alan that she was being held against her will and needed rescuing. His mind made up, he made the hand signals to express that when the sun dropped further in the sky, he would sneak around behind her and untie the knots holding her in place. She nodded, acknowledging that she understood his plan. He thought about moving now to the point behind her and waiting there for sunset but changed his mind. He thought he may have to signal her again if the plan had to change unexpectedly. It seemed that she wasn't going to take her eyes off him until she had to either.

Alan sat down under a tree and tried to put his hunger and thirst aside so he could think clearly. He thought about what must be happening back at the prison when they discover him missing. No matter how much he tried concentrating, his thirst kept overriding his thoughts. His tongue felt thick in his mouth, and his throat itched. He wanted to clear his throat or cough, but he didn't dare. Which only made it harder to endure.

What if the men decide to move on before nightfall? How would I get her away from them then?

Alan put these thoughts aside, closed his eyes, and leaned back against a tree and rested.

If they decide to leave, it will wake me, he thought.

Alan awakened with a start. At first, he didn't realize where he was, then everything that happened came flooding into his mind. It was now dusk, and as he looked into the camp of the men and their captive, he was relieved. Two of the men were lying down, and the other one was just rolling out a fur to lie on. As he watched, the third man also lay down. It was too dark to tell if the girl was looking at him or not. He moved back slowly into the woods and turned again to his left, but this time, he didn't emerge from the trees until he was directly behind the captive girl. He cautiously started forward, and as he got close to the girl, he could hear his heart beating in his chest. It was so loud he felt everyone in the camp could hear it, but no one stirred. Finally, he made it to the post, reached around, and tapped the girl on the shoulder. She didn't jump or start at all. It appeared that she knew exactly where he was at all times. She just nodded her head as she did before. Alan reached for the ropes that bound her wrists. Suddenly, the three riding beasts made a loud bleating noise, shattering the silence. Alan was taken so off guard that he fell backward onto his butt. He climbed to his feet, and just as he regained his footing, he saw one of the men heading his way at a dead run.

He was surprised that he hadn't noticed earlier that this man was built like a professional bodybuilder. As he approached, every muscle in the man's body flexed like iron cords. Alan could tell that the man meant to wrestle him, and if he succeeded in getting ahold of him, the battle would be over quickly. Alan spun with a roundhouse kick to the head but missed, going right over the man's head. Luckily, the man was so surprised at Alan's fighting style that he just stood there, looking at him. In that instant of pause, Alan remembered what wizard Azterl said, "When you see an opportunity, take advantage of it."

That was just what he did. He threw a front snap kick to the man's chin, and this time, he didn't miss. The man fell to the ground hard and unconscious. Alan didn't get a second to gather himself before the second man jumped on his back. He leaned forward while reaching over his head and pulling on the man's hair. The man was flipped completely over Alan's head, landing hard onto his back. The impact of the landing forced the breath from the man's lungs. Alan gave him no time to recover. He dropped onto one knee and threw a straight punch into the man's breastbone, shattering it with the force of his punch. The man died with pieces of bone ripping through his heart and lungs.

Before Alan could get to his feet, he heard the third man right behind him. He glanced over his shoulder for a split second, dropped his hands to the ground in front of him, and kicked out with his right leg. The back kick landed directly in the center of the man's throat. The man's thorax was crushed instantly. He was dead before he even hit the ground.

Alan stood up, just as the man who was knocked out, was climbing into the saddle of one of the riding beasts. The man urged the animal to begin running toward the trees. As Alan watched the man riding away, he immediately regretted using lethal force on the other two men. He had reacted to the surprise and uneven odds of the fight without thinking. As he watched the man flee across the clearing, he was reminded of super racing bikes on earth. The man lay on his stomach in the saddle and stretched his arms forward to hold the reins. When they reached the forest's edge, he understood the reason for riding like that. The beast's antenna pointed straight out in front of him. It was a good thing, otherwise he wouldn't have had any eyes left. The branches of the trees whipped by barely inches above the beast and rider as they ran through the forest.

Alan's attention returned to the girl. He went to her and bent down to untie her hands. He helped her to her feet and worked at untying the gag. As he pulled it away, she spat out a big piece of the fruit that the men had been eating. He noticed it was the center part of the fruit, which the men had thrown away to the riding beasts. As soon as the fruit hit the ground, the girl spoke in a deep, aged, voice of a man, "*Keiv khar toum!*"

Alan immediately found himself stiff and unable to move. None of his efforts to move would make his muscles react. It was as if he was frozen in a block of ice, without the cold. He could think and see, but he was unable to move around. The image of the girl then transformed into a man before his eyes. He still had long silver hair, but he was now very old. He was dressed in a crimson robe that reached to the ground. Alan was sure this man was a wizard. The wizard walked out of his field of vision toward the men that lay on the ground.

"A mighty fine job of killing, even if it was a little strenuous on your part. I find it so much easier to kill with words."

The wizard walked back into Alan's line of vision and stood in front of him.

"You are a tall one, aren't you? What's your name? Oh, silly me, you can't talk, can you? Well, we'll fix that. *Kapok kale!*"

Alan's head was suddenly back to normal, he could move his eyes and mouth. With the ability to move his head, it brought back his terrible thirst.

Alan said, "Excuse me, Mr.—"

"Kasan," responded the wizard.

"Okay, Mr. Kasan, could I please get a drink of that water? I haven't had a drink all day."

"Thirsty, are you? Well, I don't trust letting you loose just yet. Let me see what I can do about your thirst. *Kyushu*! There, that should do it. How do you feel now?"

Alan's thirst was gone, and for that, he was relieved. He didn't like this wizard or his stupid immobility spell, but out loud, he said, "Better, thanks."

He thought out loud, about the entry in the book, "Azterl did say, things may not always be as you see them. I guess I should have remembered that."

"How do you know Azterl?"

Alan realized he had made a mistake, speaking his mind out loud, but simply said, "Only that he is a powerful wizard of Azor."

"Powerful wizard? Ha! He couldn't even keep himself alive. He's been dead going on twenty years now. If you want to talk about powerful wizards, Krem is the most powerful wizard in Azor and always has been. He has kept himself alive since the beginning of time."

Alan asked, "Is he a friend of yours?"

"Friend? He is my father. We will go see him in the morning, and you will show him that fighting style of yours. For tonight, we will rest."

Alan questioned, "Why did those men have you held captive?"

"Those men are in Emperor Azcob's army. They captured me while I slept and stuffed that disgusting fruit in my mouth before I could speak a spell. They were bringing me to Azcob, to use as leverage against my father, so he would cease his attacks on the emperor's people."

"But how come I saw you as a woman? Is that the way they caught you?"

"No, boy, I don't run around as a woman. Only you saw me as a female. You appear to have such a weak resistance to magic. I was able to make you see me as I wished. I was able to just think the spell. You obviously aren't from this land, or I would have had to speak a spell for it to work on you."

"What is the purpose of your father's attacks on Emperor Azcob's people?"

"Why, to capture and enslave them, boy."

Alan's suspicions were correct. He made a huge mistake by helping this man get free. The warning from Azterl pounded in his ears, "Things may not always be as you see them." He would surely pay more attention to Azterl's words next time. if there was a next time.

"Well, boy, it's almost sun up. In a few minutes, we'll be on our way."

Just then, Alan felt himself falling through the blackness again, as when he came to this land. He thought to himself, *All these wizards must travel the same way. You would think they would find a less nauseating way to travel. He could have at least given me a warning that we were taking off.*

He felt himself lying on a hard surface again, and this time, he wasn't going to open his eyes until the nausea passed. He sure wasn't in a hurry to see where he ended up either.

CHAPTER FOUR

When the world ceased spinning in Alan's head, he opened his eyes. He was disappointed to see he was back in his cell at the prison. He looked at the bright side and figured at least he wasn't held captive by the wizard any longer. He sat up and looked at his watch on the table; it read, 5:20 a.m.

He started thinking that he must have dreamed the whole thing. He couldn't understand how he could have spent a whole day and night in Azor, but only been gone a little over ten hours here. The thing that bothered him the most was the fact that his cell was exactly as he had left it. If the cops had found him missing, they would have torn up his cell, looking for evidence of how he got out.

"Dream or not, I am thirsty as heck and could eat a horse."

He got up and had a drink of water from his sink. Then he made a peanut butter and jelly sandwich, as that is all he had in his cell from the canteen.

He knew breakfast would be brought to his cell in about an hour and a half.

Just then, the guard walked by doing his hourly round. Alan stopped him and asked what time it was. His intention was to see if the guard react to him being back in his cell. The guard told him the time and commented that Alan had fallen asleep last night with his sneakers on. The guard said he thought it was funny because his wife yells at him for the same thing when he comes home drunk and falls asleep fully dressed. Alan thanked him for the time and sat back down to contemplate the situation.

"I was here all the time, so it must have been some kind of dream. But it was so real; maybe my body stays behind somehow. I was wearing the same clothes in Azor—my sneakers and jeans. My body seemed real, and my thirst sure as heck wasn't a dream. What brought me back to my body here? Could it have been the sunrise here? Can I only remain there during the hours of darkness? That must be why I had to read the entries after dark at night. Or could I be back because I screwed everything up? How could I have killed two men that I went there to help? Well, Azterl, I am sorry! You counted on finding someone to help, and I messed everything up instead. I have been dreaming of something like this happening for years, and when the once-in-a-lifetime chance comes along, I can't handle it correctly."

Alan got up with renewed faith in his plan; he would recapture Kasan and turn him over to Emperor Azcob. Hopefully, this would make up for having killed two of his men. Now he needed to focus on getting some rest. His body seemed fine, but his mind was exhausted. He ate his breakfast when the guard brought it around and then went to sleep. He woke up for lunch and went back to sleep again. At 5:00 p.m., he woke up and ate dinner. He felt refreshed and wide awake now. If everything went the same as last night and it wasn't just a dream, he would be in Azor in a couple of hours.

Now that he was rested and could think more clearly, he decided his idea of capturing Kasan wasn't a good one after all. He didn't know where to find Azcob's castle, much less, know where to find Kasan. He was pretty sure Kasan would be with his father, Krem. Alan did not look forward to meeting up with a wizard who could make himself immortal, as his powers must be unlimited.

He wasn't completely forgetting about capturing Kasan; he was just putting it off till he knew more about Azor. There was just no more room for error.

He picked up the book and admired the softness of the leather cover. He held the book tightly, almost in a manner of a pledge, as he said, "I won't let you down again, Azterl!"

Then he got an idea, "I wonder if I can take things with me?"

He knew he had arrived in Azor wearing the same clothes he had lain down in when he read the poem.

"Maybe if I just try something small, hidden in my pocket, just to test it out."

He searched his cell, looking for what best to take with him. He thought about a picture of himself on his old motorcycle. But decided against it, as it would be too hard to explain a motorcycle and a camera, if he showed it to anyone. He thought of his Walkman radio, then realized there wouldn't be any stations. He imagined how impressive it would be to let someone listen to static. He considered bringing his lighter. That always impressed the natives in movies about time travel. He remembered a movie where the guy was honored as a god when the guy lit his lighter. From what Alan had already experienced on Azor, there was no reason for heat. The temperature was perfect. In addition, the men in the camp didn't have a fire going. He gave thought to his homemade knife (shank), which he kept hidden behind the wall locker in his cell. Mostly, everyone kept a shank in case trouble erupted in the prison. He decided against the knife because he didn't want to be responsible for introducing weapons into Azor, if they didn't have any already. He reflected on the men at the camp not having any weapons.

Finally, he considered a book. *Everyone likes a good fantasy story,* he thought. He then considered that a fantasy book on Azor would be pretty boring and commonplace to the reader. He went through his collection of paperbacks and chose one called *The Hit Team*. It was a true story of an Israeli hit team getting revenge on the leaders of Arab terrorism.

With sunset now almost upon him, he stuck the paperback in his back pocket and lay down on his bunk. He got comfortable, and as a last thought, he threw the blanket over his legs and feet. This would cover the fact that he was wearing jeans and sneakers in bed.

Sunset was at 7:15 p.m. tonight, and it was now.

At 7:17 p.m., Alan picked up the book and opened it to the second entry.

Entry 2

As I promised, these entries would each pertain to your impending journey to Azor. But just this once, I will also touch upon your first journey. I am glad you made it back safely. Not to say there weren't casualties, but they are to be expected in times of war.

I know my writings may be vague and appear unhelpful. They don't show exactly when to use the information in them because my writings do not predict your future in Azor. It is difficult to explain the magical process that is woven into this book's entries. Suffice to say, they are living and changing constantly.

I recommend that you read carefully what is in each entry before invoking my spell to carry you to Azor. By now, you know that your trips only last from sunrise to sunrise in Azor. A full day and night will pass while you are away from Azor and back in your world. Hopefully, on your journey this time, you will take the right road. It is best that you learn all you can on each trip. Don't let craziness get in the way of your search for knowledge. I hope you are lucky in your lonely travels, my companion. Until you read my next entry, I wish you a safe journey.

Repeat this spell, "In the name of wizard Azterl, I invoke his death spell."

Before Alan read the spell aloud, he reread the whole entry. The only thing he saw as helpful was "Learn all you can on each trip." He had already made up his mind on that one. He didn't want to mess up again, out of ignorance of Azor and its ways. He checked to make sure the paperback was secure in his pocket and then said aloud, "In the name of wizard Azterl, I invoke his death spell."

CHAPTER FIVE

Alan was prepared for the world to fall out from under him this time, but it didn't make it any easier to deal with. He still felt dizzy and sick. When he finally felt the ground beneath him, he lay there with his eyes closed for a second or two. When he opened his eyes, he saw the yellow sky and the green clouds as he expected. He was in the same clearing with the milky white pool of water.

"Well, at least I ended up where I left off last time."

Alan looked around, almost fearing wizard Kasan had hung around. He noticed the two men's bodies were gone. There were three-toed footprints everywhere he looked. It seemed as if an army of riding beasts had come and trampled any evidence of what took place here a day before. The tracks led in and then back out, in the direction the lone rider had escaped to that night. He decided he would follow the tracks as long as he was able to. Possibly, he could explain his mistake of killing the two men if he caught up to the army.

He knelt down by the pool of water. He wasn't going to get caught thirsty again; he would fill up now and then follow the tracks. As he leaned forward to drink, something struck him hard in the side, knocking him flat to the ground. As he got to his feet, he saw an animal standing about fifteen yards away, just watching him. This creature was the size of a lion, maybe weighing two hundred and fifty pounds. It had very short gold-colored fur, large pointed bat ears, and a long monkey tail and monkey paws. As Alan stared at it, the creature just sat down in the fashion a man would sit. Its front legs hung by its sides, and its hind legs stuck out in front of him. It just sat there looking at him. Alan decided he would ignore it, get his water, and be on his way. When he knelt down again, the animal got back to his feet and just stood there. As soon as Alan cupped his hands and went to dip them in the water, the animal charged again. This time, Alan jumped out of the way just in time. The creature stopped a short distance away, then walked slowly to the pool. He leaned down and barely touched his muzzle to the water's surface. The animal started convulsing and shaking his head from side to side. He began running at an unbelievable speed around the clearing while bellowing loudly. Alan realized the animal had only been trying to protect him from drinking the poison water. It then put itself in danger to prove its point when he didn't understand. This weird-looking animal had saved him.

Alan watched the creature for ten minutes as it continued running and bellowing around the clearing. When it finally slowed down and came to a stop, it walked over to him and sat down in front of him. Alan saw that the creature wasn't panting or even breathing hard; there was no sign he had been running at all. He took a chance reaching out and scratched between its big bat ears.

"I am lucky you were here. Thank you!"

Just then, he remembered something Azterl had written, "I hope you are lucky in your lonely travels, my companion."

"I will call you, Lucky. Come on, Lucky. Would you like to be my companion on my journey?"

He started walking toward the forest, following the tracks of the riding beasts. Lucky didn't move at first, then when Alan was far enough away from the pool to satisfy him, he ran to Alan and then past him. Alan couldn't believe his eyes. When Lucky reached the first tree at a dead run, he jumped right up on a branch of the gold tree. Lucky didn't miss a step or any speed; he jumped and ran from branch to branch and tree to tree. He blended with the gold trees so well that Alan lost sight of him within seconds. He hoped his new friend wasn't leaving him.

Alan continued following the tracks the army of riding beasts had left behind, for another half hour without seeing any sign of Lucky. Just when he thought he wouldn't see the weird-looking animal again, he heard a low roar. It was coming from the tree he was passing under at that second. Sure enough, it was Lucky. He had blended in so well Alan hadn't even seen him just feet away.

He happily said, "Hello there. I thought you left me."

Lucky jumped out of the tree and came and sat at Alan's feet. Alan scratched between his big bat ears as before. Lucky definitely appeared to enjoy this, as he sat happily for a few minutes longer. "Come on, we have to get moving."

This time Lucky walked a little in front of him, and about five minutes later, they came to the edge of the woods. Directly in front of them was a path that looked as if it was heavily traveled. He could clearly see the beasts had turned right onto the path, so Lucky walked in that direction, and Alan followed.

The dirt path they now traveled on was a deep-red in color. They walked along this path with the forest on either side of them for an hour or so. Lucky would jump up into the trees and run from branch to branch for a while, then come down, and walk beside him for a while. The heavy forest ended, and the path led into the open at the base of a hill. The path broke into a left and right fork at this point. Both roads looked equally traveled.

"Which road do we take, Lucky?"

Lucky started down the road to the left, going about ten yards, then sat down on the path looking at him. Alan was trying to remember exactly what Azterl had written in his entry.

"Hopefully, on your journey this time, you will take the right road."

Alan wondered if he meant *right* as in "correct," or *right* as in "direction."

"Well, Lucky, I hate to go against your choice, but I have to take this road to the right."

He started up the hill to the right. Lucky got up and followed him. As they reached the top of the hill, he saw that the road continued down the other side and back into a forest of trees. He tried to use his vantage point at the top of the hill to see where the other path would have taken them. There was a hill blocking his view in that direction, and another hill blocked his view to the other side as well.

Alan and Lucky started down the hill toward the forest. About halfway down the hill, Lucky ran ahead and jumped back into the trees. He seemed equally capable of traveling swiftly on the ground or in the trees. Alan thought he appeared happier in the trees. He had been on the forest path another half hour when he noticed the spectacular sun was directly overhead. He heard Lucky's low roar at that moment; he appeared to be just up ahead. It took him a few seconds of studying the trees ahead of him to finally see where he was perched. Lucky jumped down and came to him.

"What is it, Lucky?"

Alan noticed a clearing up ahead to the right of the path. As they neared closer, he saw that there was a house in the clearing. It was amazingly beautiful and looked like something you would see on a movie set. It was made out of crystal or a quartz-type glass. It caught all four colors of the sun and reflected them in a way that was indescribable. The house was only the size of a summer cottage, but round with an upside down cone-type roof. Even though it was made of the glass-type material, you couldn't see inside. There was a door, but no windows. Alan wanted to get some information on whether the army had come through here and how long ago. He walked across the purple grass of the lawn, but Lucky wouldn't follow. He wouldn't step onto the lawn no matter how much Alan coaxed him to come to his side. Lucky just crossed over to the other side of the path and jumped up onto a tree. He sat there looking at Alan.

"Okay, suit yourself, but I am going to find out if we are on the right road to overtake the army."

He walked up to the door of the crystal cottage and knocked on it. For a few seconds, there was no response, then he heard a cackling laugh from deep within the cottage.

"Go away, or I will turn you into an *azdirktooth*," a shrill voice said.

"I mean you no harm. I would just like to ask you a couple questions."

"Questions smestions, oggy doggy, smilly nilly, go away!"

Alan figured whoever lived here must be crazy. He wasn't going to get help here. He started to turn to leave when Azterl's words came back to him. "Don't let craziness get in the way of your search for knowledge."

"Did that mean to leave this crazy person and move on? Or does it mean that I shouldn't allow this person's craziness deter me from seeking knowledge from her?"

He wished Azterl's entries weren't so vague, as there always seemed to be more than one way of interpreting them.

He made up his mind quickly. He would insist on talking to this person. If he got nowhere, then he would move on. He turned back around and knocked a second time.

"What, you haven't gone yet! Leave an old woman to herself. Be off with you now!"

"I am not leaving until you talk to me, so if you're going to turn me into something, then do it already."

He didn't know what the creature was that she had threatened to turn him into, but he was sure it wasn't good. He had to call her bluff and see what he could find out. The day was half gone, and he hadn't accomplished anything on this trip yet. A few minutes passed with no answer. He wondered if she was calling his bluff, figuring he would just leave. He thought maybe she was cooking up the spell she promised to cast on him.

The door opened abruptly, and standing there was a very old woman. She was bent over from age, and her skin was even paler than the other people he had seen here so far. She must have been a hundred years old, or older. With silver hair as long as wizard Kasan's was, she had gold eyes with a special sparkle of youth in them. She was smiling, which eased Alan's mind a little bit, even though she was looking him up and down, as if sizing him up.

"You young azkibitz have no respect for an old woman's peace and solitude."

"I am sorry, ma'am. I didn't mean any disrespect. I am a stranger in this land, and I am in need of information."

"I'll say you are a stranger, with that yellow hair and blue eyes. Whoever thought of such a thing? You are a giant. I bet you came from the east, didn't you?"

Alan figured the sun rose in the east and set in the west here also, so he said, "Yes, ma'am, I came from the east."

"Well, I figured. There's only been tell of one person in Azor who is as tall as you. That person is Emperor Azcob. He came from the land in the east also. Do you know him?"

"I don't think so, ma'am, but my land is a very big place, and it would be impossible to know everyone."

"Yes, I guess you are right. Well, come in and sit a spell and ask your questions. Please quit calling me ma'am. My name is Azmora."

"Pleased to meet you, Azmora. My name is Alan."

"What a peculiar name."

"What's so peculiar about my name? It is a common name in my land."

Azmora just shook her head and turned, walking into her cottage.

"Sit down. I will make us something to drink, and we will talk more."

Alan followed her into the cottage and noticed why there were no windows. From the inside, it was a glass house. You could see the yard, path, and forest perfectly, right through the walls. He could even see Lucky sitting in the tree across the path if he squinted. It reminded him of two-way mirrors. The cottage consisted of only one room; it was huge. He wondered if it was a spell that made the cottage look smaller from outside, or the material it was made of. The area of the room Azmora was now in was lined from floor to ceiling with curved shelves. The shelves were jam-packed with bottles and jars of every size and shape. There was a small table encircled by four chairs, all of which were made of the same material as the cottage. She was pouring a pink liquid into two glasses at the table. On one side of the great room was a bed with a heavy dark fur as a mattress. On the opposite wall was another glass bed, minus the fur mattress. By this bed was a glass table that would have been about chest-high to Azmora. Neatly laid out on the table were an assortment of glass instruments.

"I am a doctor, if that's what you are wondering. Not that I have many patients out here. Come, sit down, and drink with me."

She motioned toward one of the chairs and set a glass of juice on the table in front of it. He wasn't sure that the small glass chairs would be able to hold his weight, but as he sat and tested it, he found it to be very strong. He took a sip of the liquid; it was thick, syrupy, and far too sweet. He was thirsty though, and it did quench his thirst.

"Thank you."

"You are welcome. Now, young *azkibitz*, what questions do you wish me to answer?"

All of a sudden, his mind was blank. He couldn't think of what he wanted to ask her. He remembered the army. But what he did ask was "That's the second time you called me a young azkibitz. What is that?"

"*Hmmm*, an azkibitz you say. Well, they are an animal that is rarely seen in Azor anymore. Wizard Krem and his evil sons hunt them and have killed most of them for sport. There may not be any left actually. I haven't seen one for years. They were large, gold, friendly creatures with big ears. They once ran through the trees by the hundreds. How I used to love watching them."

Alan realized that by calling him a young azkibitz, she was saying the equivalent of calling him a young pup. She had described Lucky to a tee. *He must be an azkibitz and probably one of the last ones alive,* he thought.

"I can assure you there is at least one azkibitz left in the forest. If you look very carefully up in the trees across the path, you will see one."

"Well, I'll be an old woman. It is an azkibitz! Is he yours?"

"No, he is my traveling companion. He saved me from drinking poison water about three or four hours east of here. I call him Lucky. I am lucky he was around."

"I'll say you are. All the water in Azor has been poisoned for years. Krem put a spell on the water, in retaliation for Azterl's spell, which changed all the trees to gold."

"Why would Azterl turn all the trees to gold?"

"Krem was using gold to entice good and honest citizens to fight against the old emperor of Azor. By turning the trees to gold, it became worthless, and the truly good people went back to the right side. Krem was so angry he poisoned all the water."

"How is it that you speak English?"

"English? I speak Azorian, as do you."

This puzzled him a little. He retrieved the book he had brought with him from of his pocket.

"Do you know how to read, Azmora?"

"What do you take me for? A fool! An idiot! Of course, I can read. Why?"

"Would you read to me from this book?" He handed it across the table to her. She took it into her hands and stared at the cover.

"What is this picture on the cover?"

"That is an Uzi submachine gun. Never mind. You don't want to know. Suffice to say it is an instrument of very evil magic."

"What is this writing? It isn't Azorian."

"I didn't think so. Azterl's spell must have given me the ability to speak and understand Azorian."

"How do you know Azterl?"

He tried to explain to her that he was from a place called earth, and wizard Azterl sent a magic book to his land, with a summons for help. He related to her the story of how sending the book, caused Azterl's death. This brought both surprise and sorrow to her face, but she sat quietly listening to his story. He told her as much as he thought she would understand. He left out that he had to return to earth at sunrise. He told her most everything else about the fight at the meadow and his mistakes. He also told her how he was tracking the army. She listened intently until Alan completed his story. She got up then and poured both of them more of the juice. She walked to a sliding ladder and climbed up to a high shelf. She took down a jar from the shelf and put some of the contents on a plate. She set the plate in front of him and said, "Eat."

The stuff looked like some kind of mushrooms that were blue, with orange dots on them. Alan nibbled one, just enough to taste it. It was spongy but sweet and quite tasty. It tasted similar to white chocolate. He wolfed down half the plate before remembering his manners.

"I am sorry for rushing like a pig. I didn't realize how hungry I was."

"Go ahead and eat, young azkibitz. I will tell you the history of Azor. I have a feeling that before you are finished with your journey, you will go through some tough times. If you are going to be of any help to Azor, you had better know as much about it as possible."

Alan finished the plate of mushrooms and sat back to listen and learn.

"Well, where do I start?"

"How about the beginning?" Alan suggested.

"Yes, the beginning."

CHAPTER SIX

"Legend has it that two men created Azor. They were both from another land that wasn't magic-oriented. As a matter of fact, the practice of magic resulted in rather deadly penalties. The two men were the best of friends. Their names were Azterl and Krem." She noticed the look on Alan's face when she mentioned those names as best friends. "Does that surprise you?"

"Well, in a way yes, but I remember Kasan saying his father has kept himself alive since the beginning of time. I guess he wasn't just boasting."

"No, Krem has his six hundredth birthday coming up. That is why he has stepped up his attacks on Emperor Azcob. But I am getting ahead of myself. Where was I now?"

"They were good friends."

"Oh yeah, for some reason, they were forced to flee the area they lived in. While hiding out in that land, they talked of a place where a person could live peacefully. Somewhere without dire penalties for practicing magic. It is told that they were both good and honest men back then. With the strength of their combined magic, they were able to create Azor. Both men passed back and forth between Azor and their homeland. They could only accomplish this together, working as a team. The reason for the trips was to find others who might be persecuted for practicing magic. They offered these people a chance to travel to and then live in a city called Azkrem. The name of the city being a combination of the two men's names.

"Let me go back just a minute. I am old, and my memory isn't what it used to be. Okay, when they first created Azor, it was a combined agreement of what the lay of the land would be. When it came time to create the villages, they couldn't agree. They moved on to creating the animals and disagreed then also. Again, they disagreed when it came to naming both the animals and villages. After not being able to come to an agreement on any of it; they eliminated all they had created to that point. Now they would start again, and Krem would create all the villages, and all but one animal. He would name one village as well. Azterl would name all the animals and all the villages, except one. He would also get to create his one animal. This compromise was possible because they both knew nothing would happen without the other's help. Together, they finally created Azor as you see it today.

"Now it was time to populate Azor, as I said before. They chose Azkrem to be the capital of Azor, as it was named after both of them. Their trips back and forth to populate Azor with suitable people was a slow and difficult process. Then sending the people they did find was taxing, even with their combined magic powers. It took some few years to populate Azkrem with one hundred people. When they came back to Azor themselves, the realization of their dreams coming true brought their friendship back to its original strength.

They didn't rule the people; there were no rulers or elite. They would play the role of judge in minor disputes, to keep the peace. In time, they both decided to find a love interest. The population of Azor had tripled by this time, so there were many women to choose from. But as fate would have it, they both chose the same woman. When this became obvious, they proposed a deal. They would both court her and let her decide. Her name was Rhea, and she was desired by many men in Azor. She was arguably the most beautiful woman in the land. When both Azterl and Krem began courting her, she was in distress. She liked them both very much. She knew the day would come when she would have to make her decision. Until then, she would enjoy the attention and company of both men. Rhea's favorite thing to do was to go out riding her *azdwark* in the country. She did this often with both men."

"I don't mean to interrupt you, Azmora, but what is an azdwark?"
He assumed it would be one of the riding beasts the army rode.
"They are the beasts you said you saw by the pool."
"Yeah, I thought so, thanks."

"Well, anyways, one day Azterl and Rhea were out riding. The azdwarks love nothing better than running, and that day they were getting their share. Azterl and Rhea were racing their mounts down this very path in front of my cottage. Rhea was leading Azterl by five azdwark lengths. She sat up in the saddle and looked back at him with a joyous laugh, her hair flowing out in the wind. As she turned forward in her saddle, the wind caught her hair and whipped it into her eyes. For a split second, she was blinded. A branch was hanging out into the path, and she ran right into it. It swept her from her saddle, and she hit the ground hard. When Azterl halted his azdwark, he dismounted and knelt beside Rhea. He knew she would live for only moments. He cradled her head in his lap trying to comfort her in her final moments. When she died, something died in him also that day. He sat in the road hugging her dead body and cursed the wind that caught her hair and caused her death. Since that day, no breeze had been felt beneath a thousand feet. That was why the clouds move, but you feel not a whisper of breeze.

"When Krem found out that Rhea was dead, he blamed Azterl for causing Rhea's death. He even went so far as accusing Azterl of creating the accident because he knew Rhea was going to choose Krem as her husband. From that day on, they never spoke to each other again.

"Azterl moved away to the empty city of Azing, and Krem went to the city he had named Kreal. The inhabitants of Azor became distressed, as they knew it was the combined magic of both men that kept Azor alive. The people traveled to both Azing and Kreal, in an attempt to reunite the wizards. Both Azterl and Krem adamantly refused to be reconciled. The people returned to Azkrem with heavy hearts and a feeling of impending doom.

"In time, Azterl sent a message to the people by *azrenit*. Before you ask, an azrenit is a sort of courier bird. You will see one eventually. Anyways, the azrenit brought Azterl's message to the people. He informed them that the reason Azor had not waned since the separation of him and Krem is because it now existed on the power of its people. He told them of the immense power that their dreams and love of freedom encompassed. As time passed, problems arose in

Azkrem, with no one to mediate. It was the decision of the people to appoint a wise man as emperor to diffuse and discern. The present emperor is Azcob. He is the man I spoke of earlier coming from the east.

"After some years, Azkrem became overcrowded, and people started drifting out to the empty villages, which Azterl and Krem had originally created throughout Azor. The town of Azing where Azterl lived was eventually populated, and he married and had children. His firstborn was a boy named Azop. Then his daughter, Aztrion, was born. Both children are wizards of limited ability. Azterl was able to remain young and alive with the aid of his magic, but the curse of that is, he outlived his wife. She died after a full life of peace and happiness.

"Krem, on the other hand, never married. He brooded, becoming more and more bitter, until it poisoned his mind completely. He kept himself alive for one reason. to see the destruction of Azor. If he, the creator of Azor couldn't be happy, why should others reap the benefit of his creation? Adding to his anger, he eventually had to accept that his strength wasn't enough to defeat the power of the people's dreams and love of freedom. The very reason he helped create this land was the thing standing in his way of destroying it. He couldn't accept that Azterl and his children weren't factors in the people's strength, so he decided to have children of his own. He used women to bear his children, then he cast the women out. His oldest was a son he named Kalem. Then by another women, he bore a girl he named Krhea. He felt it only fitting that Rhea's namesake, be an instrument of destruction of Azterl and Azor. But even with Kalem's and Krhea's powers joined with his, he wasn't successful. He had a third child by yet another woman and called this boy Kasan. Still, he was unsuccessful at destroying Azor.

"He started to believe that maybe the people's dreams and freedoms were what kept Azor alive. He came up with a plan and set it into action. His plan consisted of enslaving the people, and in so doing, he would kill their dreams and freedoms, and eventually, Azor would wither and die. The plan, he knew, would take time, but he wanted revenge on Azterl at all cost. He even took his sons out on hunting trips, in an attempt to eliminate every azkibitz from Azor since that was the one animal Azterl created."

"Do you think Lucky is the last azkibitz in Azor?" Alan asked.

"I would guess he is, or one of the last. Let's hope there are others."

"When Lucky and I arrived at your cottage this afternoon, he refused to step foot on your lawn, no matter how much I coaxed him. Why was that?"

"To answer that, I will have to share a little history of my life. Would you like some more juice? My throat is a little dry from all this jabbering. I haven't talked this much in ages, except to myself, mind you."

"Yes. More juice would be nice, thanks."

Azmora refilled both their glasses, took a long drink of her own, and sat back down to finish her story.

"Azterl and I were friends of a sort. I delivered both his children, back when I lived in Azing. As I grew older, I wished to get away from the hustle bustle of village life. I mentioned this to Azterl one day, and he offered to conjure up this beautiful cottage for me. The tree that caused Rhea's death used to stand where my front yard is now. I think he meant for this amazing building to be a permanent monument in her memory. I also believe, had there been a doctor present that fateful day, she may have lived, or at least, we'd like to think so. He was a very good and kind man. That is why your news of his death is one of such sorrow for me. He has not been seen, or heard from, in twenty years. Deep down, most of the people of Azor pray that he only went into seclusion to build his strength. His readiness for the big battle against Krem is crucial to the people's confidence. I think it is best that you let the people of Azor think he still lives. It won't hurt anything if you keep your secret, right?"

"I will, if you think it best."

"I do!"

"But why wouldn't Lucky step—"

"Oh yeah, I forgot. When Azterl made this place for me, there were a lot of azdirktooths in this area. Before you ask, an azdirktooth is a very vicious, carnivorous, wild animal. Just hope that you never get the unpleasure of meeting up with one. As I was saying, there were a lot of them here, so Azterl put a spell around the cottage and lawn to deter animals from coming too close. No more questions now, young azkibitz. I am an old woman, and my vocal cords aren't what they used to be. I do have a couple suggestions for you though. If you wish to travel through Azor without causing a huge ruckus, I recommend you cover that yellow hair. I have some black aztrin grease that you could rub into your hair. It will wash out easily, but I think it best. You are pale enough to pass, even though you aren't as pale as the rest of us."

Alan grinned at that, thinking that being locked up continuously in the prison was good for something.

"We can't do anything about your height, or the color of your eyes for that matter."

Alan thought of the colored contacts that you could get back on earth. He couldn't get them from the prison, even if they made gold contacts. Everyone he met so far in Azor had gold eyes.

"You must have an Azorian name also. Alan just won't do. History tells, that in the beginning of time, everyone had different and odd names. When the war started between Azterl and Krem, people started using Az or K, in front of their names. This declares their loyalty. We know your loyalty lies with Azterl, so let's name you. What is your land in the east called?"

"Massachusetts!"

"A little long, don't you think?"

"How about Earth?"

"Okay, Azearth it is, young azkibitz. Now would you give an old woman the pleasure of reading to her from that book of yours?"

"Of course, I will," answered Alan.

He reached out and picked the book up off the table and started reading to her. He had to stop often to explain what certain things were like an elevator, a car, the Olympics. It was slow-going, but he managed to read three chapters. He noticed it was only about a half hour till sunrise. They had talked and then read all afternoon and through the night.

"Well, I must be on my way, Azmora. I appreciate your hospitality and all the history of Azor. Please know that it will make a difference."

"Hold on a minute, and I will get you that black aztrin grease."

She got up and took a small jar from one of the shelves and handed it to him.

"Thank you, Azmora. Oh yeah, I almost forgot. I was following the footprints of the army from the pool of water. Did they happen to pass by here in the past two days?"

"No, they would have taken the road to Azkrem, which was to your left back at the fork. Be careful on your journey, Azearth, and come back and read to me sometime. I find that story such an adventure."

Alan handed her the book, "Hold it, until I return."

He leaned over and kissed her on the cheek.

"Thank you again, Azmora."

"Oh, get on with yourself, young azkibitz." She pushed him playfully toward the door. Alan could tell her cheeks had reddened, and there was moisture in her eyes. He let himself out into the Azorian night and headed across the lawn to the path. When he stepped onto the path, he was surprised by Lucky jumping out of the tree and running up to him. Alan scratched behind Lucky's ears as they walked.

"I am sorry I left you alone so long, Lucky, but I am going to leave you again in a few minutes."

Alan went to a tree on the side of the path and hid the jar of grease behind it. He sat down, and Lucky came and sat beside him. He scratched Lucky's head and then the sun broke just a sliver of light into the world of Azor. He felt the world drop out from under him.

CHAPTER SEVEN

The fall through the black nothingness was just as sickening as usual. No matter how many times he experienced it. The worst part was the feeling of fear that he would get stuck in the nothingness, just falling, falling forever.

Since he had to keep his eyes closed for a while once he felt something under him, he thought about what Azmora had told him. He also thought about what the hundred people that first went to Azor felt about the fall through nothingness. They must have felt that they were tricked by the devil himself and were falling straight into hell.

Finally, the spinning stopped in his head, and his stomach felt mostly back where it should be. He reluctantly opened his eyes to find himself back in his cell. It was only 5:25 a.m. and perfectly quiet in the cellblock. Normally, the noise in the block could drive you crazy. The block he was in had forty-five cells, with fifteen cells to each of the three tiers. The front of the cells were bars, similar to an animal cage at the zoo. The measurements were nine feet from front to back, six feet from side to side, and the ceiling was eight feet high. Looking into the cell, the metal table was attached to the right wall. There was a seat connected to the table that could be swung out to sit on and swung under when not in use. Alan's table had no seat; it was most likely torn from the table by an angry occupant sometime in the past. He was probably expressing his anger and frustration with a guard not doing his job or withholding something the inmate was entitled to. Such problems literally arose on a daily basis. At least 90 percent of the time it was caused by the guard's laziness or just plain evil intentions. The reasons behind these types of incidents could range from something as simple as a piece of mail or as serious as a life-threatening medical issue. Such a situation would result in all the men rallying together to make as big of a disturbance as possible. Forty-five angry men could make one heck of a ruckus. Oftentimes, getting a nurse or the captain to the block to address the issue was the only recourse the men had. When the guard on duty refused to acknowledge the issue, the inmates had to get someone's attention to make the guard do his job. The usual mode of noisemaking was banging the table seats into the wall the table was attached to. The bed was on the opposite wall from the table. The men would sit on the bunk sideways while bracing their hands on the bunk, and they would kick the seats. The seat would smash into the wall and recoil on its swinging arm, right back into the inmates' next kick. The noise this produced would literally reverberate throughout the prison. Add to this, forty-five men screaming profanities at the top of their lungs, and you had a literal madhouse. If it was necessary for this behavior to go on for more than a half hour, the other blocks would join in just to get a response and give their heads a break. This "ripping out," as it is called, resulted in the higher-ranking officers showing up to find out the cause of the disturbance. Other reasons for ripping out were showers not being given, food portions missing from trays, and any number of grievances. The men in lockdown were allowed three showers a week, and a man could get pretty upset when he is denied one of the few he has coming.

There were degrees of ripping out also; sometimes, it got real crazy, and the men decided that their grievances weren't being dealt with. The men would step it up, by clogging their toilets and flushing them nonstop. The guards had to get the keys for the crawl space located behind the cells. Then they had to go to each of the forty-five cells and individually turn off the water. If you had ever had your toilet back up in your house, that one flush could make quite a watery mess. Imagine forty-five toilets flushing continuously for a half hour, and these toilets don't have refill tanks. The end result was the guards doing three or four hours of water cleanup when they could have resolved the initial issue in just minutes. Suffice to say, intelligence wasn't a prerequisite in the hiring of guards.

Anyways, Alan's table had no seat, but eventually he was able to acquire two milk crates set on top of one another as a seat. On the back wall was a stainless steel sink. The sink had a water spout exactly like the water bubblers they had in school hallways—the ones where you had to just about put your lips on it because the arc of water was so short. This made washing and shaving in the sink almost impossible. To add to this, the sink was equipped with separate hot and cold buttons that had to be pushed and held for the water to continue running.

On that same back wall was a stainless-steel toilet. If you thought a ceramic toilet was cold, you'd never want to sit on a stainless steel one. There was also a small shelf for cosmetics and under this shelf were four hooks to hang clothes.

The other things you were allowed in the cell, depending on your status and which cellblock you are housed in are a thirteen-inch television, a table radio, or Walkman radio. The items were sold by the prison without speakers, so you had to use headphones for everything. You could have an eight-inch fan. The clothes allowed were two pairs of pants, two shirts, five underwear, T-shirts, and socks. Footwear was limited to a pair of sneakers or boots.

The laundry was picked up once a week. You placed everything into a fishnet-type bag and tie it closed. All the bags were washed together in industrial washers and dryers. The clothes remained in the bag until returned to you, usually half washed and still wet. Basically, you got back a ball of wrinkled wet clothes.

You were allowed to buy a limited amount of food and cosmetics from the canteen each week. You obviously needed to have money available in your prison account to make these purchases.

In the maximum-security prison, you weren't allowed any heating utensils like a hot pot or stinger. This makes it difficult to have a cup of coffee, or make a ramen noodle soup, which they sell you. The hot water from the sink just wouldn't do. The inmates were quite creative and came up with ways to get around most issues. When a prisoner wishes to heat water, he would take a milk carton like the small ones you get in the school cafeteria. The prisoners got these with breakfast. They opened the top and tie a string through two holes poked in the top to hold it. Then they filled it with water and held it above an open flame until it boiled. The open flame was produced by a thing called a doughnut. A doughnut was made by wrapping a large amount of toilet paper around your hand, sliding it off, and tucking the edges in like a hem. The result was a paper doughnut. The doughnut was lit in the center and burned a single flame like a Bunsen burner. The milk carton wouldn't burn for some reason, but it usually was only used once and then thrown away.

Most of the guys in the prison had the bare minimum of property, due to the fact that ripping out resulted in disciplinary reports being written against them. The sanction then handed out was loss of canteen or their property, such as television, radio, etc. for up to months at a time. Each rip-out session would result in cumulative sanctions.

Under normal circumstances, the noise level in the block could be aggravating, to say the least. The men yelled from cell to cell when holding conversations. Some men played chess on homemade paper chessboards yelling the moves out to one another. Each man had a board and moved his pieces and his opponent's pieces, as they were yelled out. A lot of arguments resulted from differences of where the pieces should actually be on the board. The result of all this was a constant loud buzz in the cellblock.

Alan figured he would take advantage of the quiet in the block to think about some of the stuff that confused him about Azor.

One of the things he wished he had asked Azmora was, Why didn't Azterl use his magic to heal Rhea? Then he thought about Azmora being a doctor. If the wizards' magic could heal people, then you wouldn't need doctors. Azmora was certainly sixth or seventh generation born on Azor. So there must have been a need of doctors right from the beginning, and the art was passed down from generation to generation. Satisfied he had come up with a reasonable answer to that question, he went on to the question of where Azterl and Krem originally came from.

Krem was having his six hundredth birthday on Azor in a short while, and that would make him three hundred earth years old. If the wizards were from earth originally, that would place them around the year 1691.

Isn't that close to the time they were hanging and burning witches in Salem, Massachusetts? he thought to himself.

He reflected on Azmora's telling of the history of Azterl and Krem and how there were dire penalties in their land for practicing magic. You couldn't get much more dire than hanging or burning.

The rest of the people he had witnessed in Azor could be from earth, other than a couple of minor things. He wondered if witches even had that kind of power in the days of Salem, or even now for that matter. He tried to remember what they taught about the Salem witch trials. From what he could remember, the whole thing was made up by some silly girls looking for attention, and it caused many innocent lives to be taken. Maybe there were some incidents based in truth that caused the fear and persecution. Just maybe Azterl and Krem were part of those incidents and escaped punishment. It really came down to what you believe, just like his present situation was based on believing.

If the people were from earth, then why were there differences in their appearance? He thought, *If they did come from earth, all one hundred and two of them, there would be variation. Some would be tall or short and have different eye and hair colors. It would be impossible to find that many people, five-foot tall, with black hair and gold eyes.* Alan had never even heard of gold eyes or anything close. He wondered what caused the changes, if they were from earth.

This started quite a question-and-answer session with himself.

"I will take each thing, one at a time, and see if I can find logical answers. Okay, first the black hair and silver hair. The silver could be the normal result of age. But what caused it all to turn black to begin with?"

He got out of his bunk, turned on the light, and found his dictionary, as it was the only source of information he had at hand.

He continued his self-conversation, "Would melanin have anything to do with hair, or is it just skin color?"

He looked up *melanin*—"a dark pigment found in the skin, retina, and hair."

He then looked up *pigment*—"a substance such as chlorophyll or hemoglobin that produces a characteristic color in plant or animal tissue."

Not much help in that, he thought.

He delved further and looked up *chlorophyll*—"a green plant pigment essential in photosynthesis."

And then he looked up *hemoglobin*—"the oxygen-bearing, iron-containing protein in vertebrate red blood cells, consisting of about 6% heme and 94% globin.

"Well, if I were a scientist, I might just understand this."

He decided to look up *heme*—"the nonprotein, ferrous iron-containing component of hemoglobin having composition of $C_{34} H_{32} N_4 O_4 Fe$.

"Yeah, that sure helps me!"

He tried another word: *globin,* but it wasn't there. He found *globulin*—"any of a class of simple proteins that are found in blood, milk, muscle, and plant seeds."

"Well, let's see if I can make anything out of this mess. Maybe they eat plant seeds, which contain globin, which is 96% of hemoglobin, which is a substance that produces pigment, which in turn made all their hair black over generations. It is weak but a possible answer. I don't think it would win me a Nobel Prize," he laughed.

"All right, let's give pale skin a try. This brings me back to pigment."

He caught a movement out of the corner of his eye; it was another damn cockroach crawling up the wall. He took his shower shoe from the floor and squashed the roach against the wall. He wiped the wall with a piece of toilet paper and went back to what he was doing.

"Well, let's see now, lack of pigment would produce pale skin, but that would go against my answer for the black hair. This is crazy!

"Wait a minute...

"If they did have an overabundance of pigment from eating plant seeds, it would turn their hair black, and then if there were no ultraviolet rays from the multicolored square sun, they would be pale.

"Damn, this theory is getting weaker as I go along. If I am wrong about one thing, the whole thing falls apart."

He gave the height of the people some thought. "Maybe they are all chronic smokers, and it has stunted their growth. Come on, Alan, let's get serious! Okay, let's look up *calcium*—'a silvery metallic element that occurs in bone, shells, limestone, and gypsum.'

"That isn't much help, but people always say milk makes you grow, so lack of it may stunt your growth. I don't remember seeing any cows, and doubt I will. Actually, it seems all the animals on Azor were made up in Azterl and Krem's mind."

He decided to give one more thing a try.

"All right, the gold eyes. Let's see…

"I can look up *iris*—'the pigmented, round, contractile membrane of the eye, situated between the cornea and lens and perforated by the pupil.'

"Well, here we are at pigment again. I am starting to believe I am on to something. Three of the four things that are different about these people have to do with pigment. I am not even going to guess what the cause may be, but there is something.

"Well, Alan, are these people from earth originally? I am no closer to answering that now than when I started. Maybe when I go back to Azor, I will march right up to Krem's place and ask him straight out if he's from earth. Heck, he would speak me dead before I could open my mouth.

"I wonder if this Emperor Azcob would know. Azmora said he came from the east. I should have asked her more about him.

"Did he use the book to get there? If he did, then how did he stay? Now that I think of it, Kasan said Azterl had been dead for twenty years, and Azmora basically verified that he hadn't been heard from in that long time. That would mean only ten earth years had passed since Azterl sent his book away.

"The letter I found from Mary Johnson said her father had been missing eight years. Is he Azcob? It would fit. I must go straight to Azkrem on my next trip and talk to Azcob.

"Azmora said the road to the left led to Azkrem. If I had only followed Lucky down the road he had indicated, I would have already talked to Azcob and have these answers."

The guard was just bringing around the breakfast trays, so Alan ate and fell asleep, thinking he had failed a second time.

CHAPTER EIGHT

Alan slept throughout the day, waking only to eat his meals when they were brought around. When next he woke, it was 8:15 p.m.

"Crap! I overslept. The sun had been down for an hour. That means I had missed two hours in Azor."

He reached across to his table and picked up wizard Azterl's book and opened it to the third entry.

>Entry 3
>
>I hope you are saving your luck for when you need it most. Azor is a dangerous land for an outsider. I assume you have come to this realization on your first two trips. I hope you have come up with at least an idea on how to help the people of Azor. Azor is so dear to my heart and not just because I helped create it. I am proud of what it stands for. The fact that people can live quietly and in peace, freely, is so important. I was willing to lay my life down for my world to continue on. I didn't do this out of egotism but because of the people.
>
>Magic alone cannot save Azor. I don't know exactly what can, but Krem's plan of enslaving the people can surely destroy it. I know so well what the result is of taking away people's dreams and freedoms. These are the very things I left behind in my homeland. I don't know if that world even exists any longer, but the direction it was headed

doesn't bode well for its continued existence. I pray this is not the fate of Azor.

I wish I could give you the answer, but if I knew the answer, this book would not be necessary. The ending of my life would not be necessary. I thought of killing Krem and those that helped him, but I would become what I left behind. Are the people whom Krem leads wrong or guilty of anything but loyalty to him? Just because someone loves a person and is loyal to them, doesn't mean they agree with their beliefs. I apologize for burdening you with my failure. I pray you are more successful than I, and you can succeed in saving Azor for its people.

Alan invoked Azterl's spell and felt himself falling away from the world, or the world falling from him. While falling, he realized he had been in such a hurry from oversleeping that he didn't even put his sneakers on. He wore only the gym shorts he had been sleeping in.

As he felt the ground appear beneath him, he lay there with his eyes closed. He was thinking how he would look meeting the emperor in nothing but a pair of shorts.

A familiar voice brought him back to reality. He opened his eyes and found himself lying behind the tree he was leaning against when he left Azor last. The person belonging to the voice he heard was blocked from his view by the tree. The voice and what it was saying made Alan's blood turn to ice water.

He listened while carefully getting up and then peeked, his head around the tree. What he saw was a man in a crimson robe and with long silver hair. Fortunately, his back was facing where Alan hid.

Alan's fear increased when he saw that wizard Kasan was facing Lucky. Lucky wasn't moving; he was as motionless as a statue. Alan could hear Kasan talking to the unmoving azkibitz.

"Well, what should I do with you? I could speak you into a million pieces. Or better yet, I could present you to my father and let him have the pleasure of killing you himself. We thought we had killed all of you filthy creatures of Azterl's. I think I will kill you myself."

Alan didn't wait for Kasan to make up his mind; he ran from behind the tree and crossed the ten yards separating him from Kasan. Before Kasan could react to the sound behind him, Alan landed a blow to the back of his neck, knocking Kasan unconscious. Kasan collapsed in a bundle of crimson robe to the ground. Alan went directly to Lucky, but there was no change. He was still under the effects of Kasan's spell. Alan looked around for something to gag and bind Kasan with, but there was nothing. Kasan was starting to stir. Alan went over to him and propped him up into a sitting position. He placed himself behind Kasan, with his arm around his throat in a choke hold. He didn't yet apply pressure, as he wanted Kasan awake but controlled.

When he thought Kasan might be conscious enough to speak, he tightened his grip to prevent him from talking. Alan's mouth was next to Kasan's ear, and he spoke calmly but firmly to him.

"I can kill you now if I wish, but that is not my preference. The first thing I want you to do when I release you is to take the spell off the azkibitz. You already know my magic is stronger than yours, as I broke your spell and escaped on our last meeting. If you try anything other than what I tell you, I will just disappear. You will never know where or when I will turn up again. I give you my word. The end result will be your demise. Do you understand me?"

Kasan slightly moved his head up and down, as the pressure Alan held on his neck didn't allow him much movement. Alan released his hold, stood up, and moved away from him.

"Now release the azkibitz from your spell!"

"*Kepate keline.*"

Immediately, Lucky returned to normal and ran to Alan, almost knocking him over in his excitement. Alan gave him a quick pat on the head, then turned his attention back to Kasan. He was standing there, rearranging his robe with one hand, while rubbing the back of his neck with the other.

Alan expected to be blasted into oblivion, but Kasan must have believed his bluff and just stood there, glaring at him. He wasn't sure how far he could push Kasan before he would come out fighting, and he didn't want that to happen. He knew Kasan would fight with magic.

"This is my azkibitz, and I don't want you or your family to ever think you can harm him without my killing you for it. So I suggest you make it your business to see no harm comes to him."

"How do I know one azkibitz from another?"

Alan thought about this for a second, then decided on a way to be sure Lucky couldn't be mistaken for another azkibitz, if there were any others. His idea would give him an opportunity to further bluff Kasan into thinking he had magic powers.

Alan turned toward the tree he had hidden behind and spoke the first magic words that came to his head.

"Hocus-pocus!" Alan said in a loud voice while pointing at the tree.

He then walked to the tree, reached behind it, and took the jar of black aztrin grease from where he had left it hidden. He came back toward Lucky, holding the jar, so Kasan could clearly see it.

He stood next to Lucky, opened the jar, and scooped out a glob of the grease. He set the jar down and rubbed his hands together, covering both palms completely. He then put a palm print on either side of Lucky's front shoulder muscles, like the Indians used to do to their ponies.

"Now you know my azkibitz, from any others!"

"What do you want with a dirty Azterl-created beast anyhow?"

"This azkibitz saved my life, and I, unlike yourself, repay kindness with kindness."

"I was grateful that you saved me from Azcob's soldiers. I wasn't going to hurt you. I was only going to take you to see my father."

"You attempted to take me against my will until I broke your spell and left."

"How did you break my spell? No magician in Azor can break another's spell."

"My magic is not of Azor and is much more powerful than yours."

He hoped he wasn't playing it up too strongly. He didn't want to push Kasan into a duel of magic. He just wanted to scare him enough, so he wouldn't try anything.

Kasan said, "Listen, I really didn't mean you any harm that day. I just wanted to be sure of your intentions. That's why I put the spell on you."

"Why did you want to take me to your father?"

"Only to show him your odd fighting style."

"Why would that interest him?"

"Fighting is an honored and respected sport in our land, but never have I seen such a fighter as yourself. I am ranked the tenth-best fighter in Azor myself."

This puzzled Alan; an old man like Kasan couldn't be too good in a fight.

"You kid me, right? You must be a hundred years old."

"One hundred and twenty to be exact, but I am a wizard as you are. Maybe not as strong, but that is yet to be seen. I do have enough power to keep myself alive, but I could never live as long as my father has. He is almost six hundred and will probably live four hundred more, if not forever. I might make it four hundred years in all. I only look old to you because that is how I wish to be seen. People seem to respect an old wizard more than a young one."

"*Kazak khaniz!*"

Alan heard Kasan speak the spell before he could react. All he could do was stand there and see what Kasan's spell did to him. Nothing happened to him, but something was happening to Kasan. The old wizard was dissolving before his eyes only to become a young man of about twenty-five.

He was now dressed in a crimson robe from the waist down and wore light leather boots. He still had long silver hair. His upper body completely took Alan by surprise. Kasan must have had a fifty-inch chest and twenty-inch arms, with every muscle ripped like he just worked out. Arnold Schwarzenegger would have a hard time besting Kasan in a flex-off contest, and Kasan was relaxed.

"To prove that I don't wish to deceive you in any way, I am showing you my true self."

"I can see why you are ranked so high in fighting."

"Size and strength does not always make the best fighter," Kasan said.

He continued, "For example, Azire, the man you knocked out at the meadow, is ranked number 1 in Azor, and you bested him."

Alan didn't know what to say, but he hoped his beating this Azire would make Kasan even more cautious of trying anything with him.

"I appreciate you revealing your true self to me, and I feel more confident that you aren't trying to deceive me."

Alan wasn't completely satisfied as to Kasan's motives but decided to give him the benefit of the doubt.

"Would you go with me to see my father then?"

Alan needed to get to Azkrem to see the emperor, but not in shorts and no shoes, and this opportunity may not present itself again. He made up his mind to go, in the hopes that he would find out some information to help the people of Azor.

"Yes, Kasan, I would be honored to meet the famous wizard Krem. Are you sure he won't mind an unexpected visitor?"

"I have told him of our first meeting, and he looks forward to meeting and thanking you."

"Okay, how do we get there?"

"I will call my *azreyvick*, and he will carry us to my father's castle. First, you must send your azkibitz into the forest, as azreyvicks had been trained in the hunting of azkibitz."

Alan tried to tell Lucky to take to the forest, but he just wasn't willing to leave his side.

"Why don't you use your magic on him to make him go away?" asked Kasan.

"I can't use my magic on a friend."

"Why not just walk into the woods and he will follow you. Then I will put a spell on him to freeze him there. When we are leaving, I will unfreeze him."

Alan didn't like the idea much, but Lucky refused to leave his side.

"Yes, I guess that would be all right."

Alan took a few steps into the forest, and Lucky followed right by his side. When he got about twenty yards into the woods, he stopped, knelt down, and wrapped his arms around Lucky's neck and hugged him.

"I must go with this wizard. I know you don't like him, but it is important for Azor. We shall find each other again. Azterl said I will need your help."

Alan stood up and scratched behind Lucky's ears.

"Okay, Kasan, you can use your spell now."

"*Keiv khar toum!*"

Alan heard the wizard speak the same words that had first frozen him by the pool of water, and Lucky was now immobilized. He walked out of the trees and over to where Kasan stood.

"You can call your azreyvick now."

"I have already summoned him. We control them with our mind. That is how my father wanted it when he created them."

Just then, a shadow was cast over both men. Alan looked up to see what caused it. The creature he saw actually scared him. It was a giant rat with wings. It must have weighed two thousand pounds, at least, and was the size of an earth car. Its wings were made of feathers and spanned a good forty feet across. The creature was staying aloft, just above the path and trees. The path itself was only about twenty feet across, and Alan was convinced the azreyvick wasn't going to be able to land here. Then the azreyvick folded its wings to its body and dropped out of the air onto the path in front of the two men. It landed hard and clumsily but seemed no worse for wear.

"Come on, it is a long flight to Kreal, but we should make it by nightfall."

"Why don't you just use your magic to take us to Kreal and save some time?"

"Carrying both of us that distance will tax my power more than I am willing to allow. It would be unwise to disadvantage myself like that, especially in time of war. Unless, of course, you can bring yourself, but I assume you need to be familiar with your destination in order to use your magic, right?"

Alan noticed Kasan was looking at him suspiciously, and he felt that he almost messed up.

"That is why I asked if you could take us."

Alan noticed the suspicion drain from Kasan's face when he answered.

Kasan said, "Okay, what is your name anyways?"

Alan wasn't comfortable sharing the name he and Azmora had come up with since Azearth would reveal his loyalty to Azterl.

"My name is Alan."

"What an odd name. Well, Alan, let's get started. As I said, it's a long trip to Kreal."

They approached the azreyvick, and Kasan grabbed a handful of hair and pulled himself up, climbing onto the animal's back. Allan followed suit and climbed up behind him.

He wondered how the azreyvick was going to take off being unable to spread its wings. All of a sudden, the creature started running down the path and jumped into the air.

Alan had to quickly grab handfuls of hair to keep from falling off. The azreyvick's jump was so high it carried them just above the trees' height. The animal spread its wings and flapped them hard to stay aloft. Then he stopped flapping and spread its wings, gliding away.

Alan remembered Lucky; he touched Kasan on the shoulder and said, "Will you release my azkibitz now?"

"Oh yeah, I almost forgot. *Kepate keline!*"

"Thanks."

Alan hoped that Lucky would be okay and not feel betrayed. He enjoyed the azkibitz's company and hoped to see him again.

Alan noted that they were traveling north, and they stayed beneath the thousand-foot level, so there was no wind for the azreyvick to fight against. They flew on in silence for quite some time over forests, rivers, and meadows. At one point, they flew over a village that Kasan told him was called Azmig. They flew by so quickly that he couldn't make out much about the village other than it was small.

Then about an hour later, they spied an army of about twenty of Azcob's men, along with twenty azdwarks resting in a small clearing.

"Watch this!" Kasan yelled over his shoulder.

Just then, the azreyvick dove toward the clearing and buzzed the azdwarks. The azreyvick let out an ear-splitting, high-pitched, screeching cry that hurt Alan's ears. The azdwarks took off at a dead run in the direction of the forest cover. The army of men ran after them, attempting to catch them, but they were no match for the azdwark's speed.

"It will take them hours to catch their riding beasts," Kasan said, with a laugh.

Alan didn't find it funny but said nothing.

They flew on for hours in silence until just before dusk. Alan could see the castle in the distance. It was surrounded on three sides by a village. There was a moat filled with the milky-white water, which separated the castle from the surrounding village. There wasn't enough light left for Alan to make out much detail of the village.

The azreyvick landed on one of the tower's flat roofs, which was surrounded by a parapet. Kasan and Alan climbed down off the azreyvick, stiff and sore from the many hours of flying across Azor. As soon as they disembarked from the animal, it took off and climbed away into the night sky. Alan watched it, silhouetted against the square Azor moon. He hadn't really noticed it before, but besides the moon being square, it looked just like earth's moon. It was a little brighter, maybe to compensate for the lack of stars here in Azor.

"Come on this way." Kasan motioned, heading for a lighted doorway at the other end of the tower.

Alan caught up to him as he went through and started down a stairwell. They continued down until they entered into a huge brightly lit room. The source of light must have been magic, as he could detect no other light source of any kind.

The walls were covered in gold pelts. There were literally hundreds of them. There was a round ring of some type of matting in the middle of the room. The ring reminded him of a sumo wrestling ring of earth's Japan.

"This is the fighting room. Sit down, and I will call Krhea to get us some refreshments. You must be hungry and thirsty after our flight."

"Yes, I am, thanks."

Alan went to one of the many couches that surrounded the fighting ring. As he went to sit down, it dawned on him what the gold pelts on the wall were. The couches were all covered with the gold fur also.

"Is this azkibitz hide on the couches and walls?"

"Oh, I am sorry. I forgot about your friend the azkibitz. We'll go in the other room. Come this way."

They went through a doorway and entered another brightly lit room, about half the size of the fighting room. This was obviously the dining area. In the center of the room, there was a large table with about twenty chairs around it.

They sat at the table, and Kasan called out loudly, "Krhea, are you home? I have brought a guest. Come bring us refreshments."

No sooner did he yell out than a woman walked through the door at the opposite end from where they came in. She carried a tray filled with all kinds of strange-looking fruit items. She also had a pitcher and two glasses on the tray.

She was pretty, in a plain sort of way. She seemed to be in her early thirties and had the expected long black hair. It was braided and reached all the way to just an inch off the floor. Had it been unbraided, it surely would have dragged behind her as she walked. She was a little bit overweight but carried it attractively. She was also wearing a crimson robe. Alan determined this must be the family color.

"Hello, Kasan, how was your trip? This must be the man you told us about who saved you from Azcob's army. He's the one who also broke your spell and left you standing there alone."

Alan suspected a hint of taunting in her statement, but Kasan didn't notice or acted as if he hadn't.

"Yes, Krhea, meet Alan."

"Alan, this is my elder sister, Krhea."

"Pleased to meet you and thanks for the drink."

"You are welcome, and it's a pleasure to meet you as well. Kasan has told us of your beating Azire, as well as killing the two other soldiers of Azcob's army. My father and elder brother, Kalem, have been looking forward to meeting you. It is with regret that they are out at the time. I am not sure when they will return."

"I am sure they will return before morning." interjected Kasan.

"I hope so. I was hoping to speak with the wizard of Kreal."

"And he with you, I am sure. Until then, let us get some rest. That was a trying day. Also, my neck hurts." Kasan winked at Alan.

"Come, follow me, and I will show you a place you can rest." motioned Kasan.

Alan turned and thanked Krhea once more before leaving. She smiled and looked down at the floor. He was sure he saw color come to her pale cheeks before she turned and shuffled off. Alan caught up with Kasan as he was leaving the dining hall. He followed Kasan up a flight of stairs that emerged onto a long hallway. They walked down the hall, passing many doors as they went along. Finally, Kasan stopped at a door that looked no different from all the others they had passed.

"Oh, here we are." Then he materialized a key out of thin air and unlocked the door.

"Hey, Kasan. I already have another room made up for our guest." Krhea had come out of nowhere.

"This room is just fine!" Kasan pushed the door open and stepped back, allowing Alan to go in.

Alan stepped into the room, and the door slammed closed behind him. He turned and tried to push against the door, but it was already locked. There was no handle on the inside. He stood there, listening to the voices on the other side of the door.

"Kasan, you are a rotten, ungrateful person. He saved you from Azcob's army. Why do you treat him as if he was the enemy?"

"Shut up and mind your business, Krhea. You sound like a weak-hearted Azterl follower."

"Alan, can you hear me?"

"Yeah, I can hear you, Kasan. You can be sure this isn't going to turn out good for you!"

"I am not too worried. This room was built by my father to hold Azterl, if he could have caught him. No magic spell can be cast from inside. But the effects of a spell cast out here can be felt by the occupant of the room. So I suggest you sit tight and not get too bold with the threats. I can cause you much pain, and you are defenseless. I will be back after I rest some. Goodbye, powerful wizard." Kasan walked away, laughing wickedly, not unlike the guard's laugh on earth.

Alan sat on the bunk in his new prison cell.

"Damn, now I am in prison in two worlds. I guess I am destined to be locked up."

CHAPTER NINE

Alan looked around the cell. It was worse than his cell on earth. This cell only had a bed, no sink, toilet, or table. He lay back on the bunk, as he couldn't think of anything better to do. He closed his eyes and thought about his situation.

"Well, I have been a ton of help to Azor so far. I can't even get out of a stupid room. If I would have just shut up and not boasted about my nonexistent magical prowess, Kasan probably wouldn't have locked me in here. Now I can't even go back to earth, with the stupid spell on this room. What will happen if the guard sees me sleeping throughout the day's meals? If they try to wake me up for a meal—oh crap, it is shower day tomorrow. They will definitely try to wake me up. I have to try to figure a way out of this cell before sunrise."

He got up and checked every part of the cell, but there was no way out. The door was solid. Knocking it down was not an option. He sat back down in defeat and waited. An hour went by when he heard footsteps coming down the hallway. The person stopped in front of his cell door.

He heard Kasan speaking familiar spells. "*Keiv khar toum, kedo.*" Then he heard "*Kapate keline, kiama,*" and lastly, he heard "*Keiv khar toum, kumi.*"

Alan found himself immobilized, standing at the door, in the position he had gotten in to strike whoever came in the door. The door opened, and Kasan stepped in. He smiled when he saw the position Alan was in.

"So you meant to strike me and escape, did you?"

The door closed of its own volition, and immediately, Alan was no longer immobilized. He stood there facing Kasan.

"I have invoked a spell before entering this room that made you unable to act. Now that the door has sealed itself we are equal because our magic is useless in here."

Alan considered why Kasan would trap himself in the cell also, but his train of thought was broken by Kasan rushing at him.

"Now you and I will fight, and I will learn to be the best fighter in Azor."

Kasan hit him in the chest with his shoulder, as if he was trying to take a door down. The blow slammed him into the wall, jarring every bone in his body. It also knocked the wind out of him.

Kasan reached down, with a laugh, and picked him up by the throat, then propped him up against the wall. Kasan tightened his grip, and Alan started to see stars.

Alan reached across and gripped Kasan's wrist in a snakelike fashion. He twisted and came up under Kasan's arm while putting his other hand on his elbow. This maneuver put Alan behind Kasan's back, holding his arm out behind him. He shoved Kasan's arm up hard behind his back while putting the arch of his foot behind Kasan's knee. He pushed firmly, and Kasan dropped to his knees with his arm painfully pinned behind his back. Alan pressed his other knee into Kasan's back, causing him to arch back in pain. He grabbed Kasan's hair and pulled his head back as far as he could so that he was actually looking down into Kasan's face inches away.

"Now, my ungracious host, you will open the door and let me out of here. I swear I'll break your arm and back at the same time."

"I can't open the door any more than you can."

"Quit your lying. You wouldn't come in here without having a way of getting out."

"I didn't say I don't have a way out. I just said I couldn't open the door. The spell I spoke before I came in not only rendered you helpless but also closed the door and locked it when I entered. After a couple hours, you will become helpless again. At that time, the door will open and then reclose when I exit. Then I will have to remove the immobilization spell from you."

"Well, you better do something."

"I truly can't do anything. That is why I spoke all the spells before entering the room. Would you please let me go now so we can continue with my lessons?"

Alan thought about letting him go and just sitting on the bed. But if he refused to fight, Kasan would just attack him again. Alan let him go, asking, "When do you plan on letting me out of here?"

"Just as soon as you teach me enough to beat Azire and become the best fighter in Azor."

Alan thought about how long it may take to teach someone martial arts and enough for it to be used in a real combat situation. Just knowing the moves wasn't going to help without repetition.

He made up his mind that he would teach Kasan blocks and trivial holds, just to buy some time. They practiced for hours, and he found himself using extra force where it wasn't really needed. He wanted to hurt Kasan without him realizing it was intentional.

Finally, Kasan's spell kicked in, and he found himself immobilized again. Kasan walked out, and the door closed tightly behind him. He heard Kasan say "*Kepate keline!*" and the spell released him.

"I will bring you some food in the morning when I get up, see ya then."

"Yeah, screw you, Kasan!"

He expected Kasan to speak a spell in response and cause him pain. But Kasan just walked away, laughing happily.

Alan lay back on the bed and realized he wasn't the only one who dished out some unnecessary pain. He drifted off to sleep.

Then in his dream state, he felt the world fall out from under him, dropping him through the nothingness. He thought he may be dreaming, but the nausea felt too real to be a dream. He made the mistake of opening his eyes right away and immediately regretted it. He had to jump up and hug the toilet. When the dry heaves finally stopped, he got up, washed his face, and brushed his teeth.

Alan sat down on his bunk, kind of glad to be in his cell here rather than his cell there. He guessed the reason for his being able to return was that he invoked Azterl's spell prior to entering the room, just as Kasan had.

"Well, I am going to end up back in the cell in Krem's castle when I return to Azor, and I won't be able to get out then either."

He decided he would think more clearly later on after some rest. Hopefully, Azterl's entry would help him in some way to deal with the cell situation. He went to sleep for a couple of hours till breakfast. Then he fell back asleep again until the guard woke him at 10:00 a.m. for his shower.

"After you get back from your shower, Eliot, pack your stuff. You are moving to Ten Block," the guard grumbled.

Alan didn't say anything. He knew there was nothing he could say, or do, to change or postpone the scheduled move. He went to the shower, then went back to pack his small number of property.

He handed off his shank to another inmate a few cells down and packed his other belongings into a small box. He put on three pairs of underwear and three T-shirts, as well as three pairs of socks. He knew when they came to move him, he would be taking only what he wore on his person. The rest of his stuff would go to the property department.

The block he was in now was the AA block; it housed guys who were on Awaiting Action status. The action they were awaiting was a departmental segregation unit board, which is referred to as a DSU board. The DSU board decides how long a prisoner should be taken out of general population and placed in segregated lockdown, or Ten Block. They make this determination based on the seriousness of the offense the person has committed in violating the rules of the institution.

Alan had been given two years in segregation. Not so much for the seriousness of the offense he committed, but because he had been "DSUed" three times previously.

He tried to figure out a way to get Azterl's book to go with him, but he knew he would be strip-searched upon arriving in Ten Block.

When the guard came to get him, he asked, "Can I bring this one book with me?"

"Sorry, Eliot, I would catch hell if I let you bring anything with you. I will see if I can get your stuff out to property today, and maybe you'll get it sooner."

AZOR'S REDEMPTION

Alan spent the first two days in Ten Block working out and fine-tuning his martial arts. He also caught up on much-needed sleep.

There wasn't that much difference between Ten Block and the AA block, except you weren't allowed to access the library in person. You could put in a request for reading material in writing, and the librarian guard would send them to you when he got around to it. The library was in such disarray that you would get whatever they sent and be glad for it.

Finally, on the third day, Alan's property was returned to him in the afternoon. He immediately looked for Azterl's book and literally hugged it when he found it. He was nervous that the property people may lose his book. They often lost people's stuff on purpose.

Alan still hadn't figured a way out of the cell in Krem's castle. He still had hope that Azterl's entry would help him. Either way, it would be a change of pace to go to Azor, even if he was stuck in a cell and had to fight with Kasan.

He was faced with another dilemma. In Ten Block, you were only allowed T-shirts, underwear, and socks of your own personal clothes. They supplied you with a tan one-piece jumpsuit and a pair of red fire-engine sweatpants. Alan had to decide which one of these he would wear on his trip to Azor.

"Won't Kasan be surprised to see me in different clothes? He won't think so much of his magic-proof cell then."

He decided on the sweatpants, as fighting with Kasan in a jumpsuit could turn out to be tough. He put on his sneakers and sweatpants at sundown and threw a blanket over him. He lay there reading Azterl's entry.

Entry 4

I hope that you are making some progress toward helping the land of Azor. I wish that Krem and I had cast spells to rid ourselves of magic powers after we completed Azor and populated it. The odds are greatly in Krem's favor as a result of his magic. His magic alone has failed to destroy Azor. If he is successful in enslaving the people and taking away their dreams, the tide will turn even more in his favor. Krem and his sons will destroy the crops in villages, and when the people are starving, they turn to Krem to get something to eat. My children do what they can to replace what Krem and his sons destroy, but their powers are limited, and it takes a lot out of them. As you now know, you can't break another wizard's spell, so you can't repair what's been destroyed. You must start from scratch. Preventive spells can be placed beforehand, but you can't predict where and when they will strike. People's ideas and beliefs are hard to change when they are presented with hard facts. Sometimes it is best to not even try. Once again, I wish you a safe journey.

Alan invoked Azterl's death spell, and once again, he experienced the fall through nothingness.

He felt the bunk beneath him and made sure he didn't open his eyes until his head settled. When he did open his eyes, he was in the castle cell as expected. There was a sour smell in the cell, and as he looked around, he saw the cause. There was a tray and fruit all over the floor. It appeared that someone had thrown the tray against the wall. The fruit was strewn across the floor, shriveled and moldy as if it had been there for days.

Alan realized that Kasan must have come to feed him, and upon finding him missing, threw the tray in anger.

"What if he doesn't come back now that he knew I was gone?"

He tried the door; it was locked tight as before. He was sure he would have to spend a day and a night here with no water or food. He paced the cell, trying to come up with options. Then he thought he heard footsteps in the hallway.

Could it be Kasan or Kalem or worse yet, it may be Krem himself, he thought.

AZOR'S REDEMPTION

Then he noticed a woman's voice singing softly, and she was approaching the door.

Should I dare try and request her help? Would she just call her brothers or father?

He made his mind up just as the footsteps reached the door.

"Krhea, is that you?"

"Yes, but who is in there? Is it you, Alan?"

"Yeah, Krhea, can you help me out of here?"

"But you were gone! I was here with Kasan when he came to feed you. Six days had gone by since then. How can it be that you are back?"

"I can't explain now. Can you open the door?"

"I can't. Kasan has the key, and unless he willingly gives it up, I can't get it."

"Can't you use your magic to get the key from him?"

"No, he has a spell on the key, and my magic cannot break his or anyone's spell."

"Would you help me get out of here, if we could get the key, Krhea?"

"Oh yes, Alan. I think Kasan was wrong in locking you up after you helped him. My father was very upset also when he came home and found out what Kasan had done. He was mostly upset because you are such a powerful wizard that you could escape the room he built to hold Azterl. He is worried you are now our enemy. My father is scared, and I have never seen him scared before. Kasan is even more scared. He thinks you will show up at any time to kill him as you promised. I don't believe you would kill him though, would you?"

"No, I guess. I wouldn't, but I would sure like to make him wish he were dead."

"You have already done that, Alan. The fact that you haven't shown up to kill him bothers him greatly."

"Yeah, I suppose it would."

"Hold on. Someone is coming. I will be back!" Krhea whispered.

He heard her shuffle off down the hall. Then he heard a heavier set of footsteps coming down the hall and pass by his door and fade away in the distance. Alan realized he had been holding his breath as he crouched quietly inside the door. A few minutes passed when Krhea's voice startled him. He hadn't heard her come back.

"That was Kalem. He was going to lie down in his room."

While Krhea was gone, a thought had come to him as he looked at the fruit on the floor.

"Krhea, could you talk Kasan into giving you the key, on the pretense of cleaning the room?"

"Oh yeah, he threw the tray when he found you missing. I will go see if he will give it to me. I will tell him the fruit smells when you pass the room. He won't be suspicious of that because I clean constantly out of boredom. I will return as soon as I can."

Alan listened to her shuffle off down the hall yet again.

"How will I get out of the castle with Kasan and Kalem home? Krem is probably here also."

He went to the bed and sat on it, waiting. After some time passed, he started worrying about what could have gone wrong. He heard the key turning in the lock, and then the door opened. Krhea stepped inside and closed the door, only leaving it open a crack.

"Sorry it took so long, but Kasan wouldn't give me the key. So I went to Father and told him about the smell. He told Kasan to clean the mess himself or give me the key. He said he wasn't running an azkibitz pen in his castle, so Kasan gave me the key, as he is lazy."

"It's a good thing he is. I wouldn't have cared for him showing up to clean the mess. Now how do I get out of the castle without your father or brothers seeing me?"

"Kalem is asleep now, so we can sneak past his room and go out the back stairs. On the tower, I will call an azreyvick to take you away."

"All right, let's go then. The sooner I get out, the better I will feel. I have had enough of being locked up in my own world."

"What do you mean by that?"

"Never mind, let's go."

They slipped out of the cell and down the hallway to a stairwell that led to a tower.

"I have already summoned the azreyvick. He will be here shortly."

"Will he take me where I wish to go?"

"You have never ridden one by yourself?"

"No, the first one I ever saw was when Kasan and I flew here on one."

"You are not from Azor, are you?"

"No, I am from the east."

"Oh, Azcob is from the east also. Did you come because of him? Are you going to help him against my father?"

"No, not really. I must see Azcob, but I came to help the people of Azor to retain their freedom."

"I think that the people should be free also, but I can't go against my father and brothers. You won't try to hurt them, will you?"

"I don't want to hurt anyone. I just want to keep peace in Azor, but I haven't done much of anything so far."

"I believe you will succeed, Alan. Where will you go?"

"To Azkrem and see Emperor Azcob."

"Have you been there before?"

"No. I haven't been able to make it yet despite my efforts."

"I am sorry. The azreyvick will not be able to take you then. They are controlled by your mind. You have to have a picture of your destination in your memory. The azreyvick sees and goes to that spot. They know all of Azor."

Alan decided he might as well go to Azmora's house since that was as far as he had seen to this point. The azreyvick arrived and landed on the tower, his long rat tail hanging over the edge of the parapet and down the side of the castle tower.

Alan remembered something from Azterl's entry—it was something about preventive spells being cast beforehand.

"Krhea, could you put a spell on me so if I met Kasan, Kalem, or your father, they couldn't use their magic against me? I promise not to harm them if I meet them along the way. It would stop them from interfering with my attempts to help the people."

"Yes, I could put a spell on you that no other wizard could break, but it would only last a day or two."

"That is good enough, please."

"*Kowto kwach, kulm!* That should do it, Alan. Why do you need my magic? You are even more powerful than my father. You broke Kasan's spell and even escaped from a cell that Azterl wouldn't have been able to."

"Can you keep a secret, Krhea?"

"Yes, I guess so."

"I have no magic powers," Alan said, as he climbed up on the azreyvick.

"Thank you, Krhea. I appreciate your help."

"You surely kid me, Alan, but I wish you luck. Goodbye."

Alan thought of Azmora's house and hoped he could control this animal. The azreyvick took off and started flying south.

"Well, at least, I am heading back the way I came."

CHAPTER TEN

As Alan flew over Azor on the azreyvick, he thought about Krhea. She seemed to be a good person. He suspected that when Krem used her to try to destroy Azor, she hadn't given her all. He wondered why she hadn't commented on his change of clothes. Maybe it was the closeness in color of his sweatpants to the family color. Possibly, she thought Kasan had given them to him.

The azreyvick flew on for most of the day. It did seem they were traveling faster than when both him and Kasan were riding. Maybe it was due to the weight difference. Alan decided he didn't want to scare Azmora by landing an azreyvick on the path in front of her house. He was sure Azterl's spell would keep it off her lawn, but he didn't have the time to spend talking with her right now, in his hurry to get to Azkrem. He changed the picture in his mind to reflect the spot he and Kasan had left from. He wondered if this was the same azreyvick or a different one. He also wondered how the beast could know one patch of path from another.

Just as he thought that, the path came into view beneath them. The azreyvick closed its wings and fell out of the sky from the height of the treetops, landing clumsily on the path. Alan forgot to hold tight and was knocked off the animal and landed hard on the path. He had to scramble out of the way to avoid being trampled by the azreyvick running down the path. It jumped into the air above the treetops, spread its massive wings, and soared away in seconds.

He got up, brushed himself off, and looked around in hopes of seeing Lucky. All he saw was the jar of black aztrin grease lying in the path where he had left it. He went a small distance into the trees to check where he had last seen Lucky immobilized. He wasn't there, so he called out a couple of times, but the silence unnerved him. He thought about the azdirktooth that Azmora had told him about. He didn't know what they looked like, but they were carnivorous, and that was reason enough not to attract one.

He walked back to the path and decided to put the grease in his hair just in case he ran into anyone. With that done, he put the jar in the pocket of his sweatpants and started down the path. He came to the fork in the path, and this time took the path to the left, which Azmora said led to Azkrem.

He walked up over the hill. The path to the right was blocked just as this one had been when he had gone to the right. At the bottom of the hill, the path ran into the forest again. He walked along the forest path for some time. A river of the milky white water ran beside the path for a period, which only made him realize his thirst. The forest ended, and the path led across a large meadow. In the distance ahead, he could see what appeared to be a large dead tree, unlike he had seen yet. As he got closer, he saw that it was actually a tree made out of wood, quite dead but still wood.

While standing beneath the tree, he heard a tiny voice. "What are you looking at? Have you never seen a tree before?"

Alan looked up into the dead branches to see where the voice had come from. He saw an animal that resembled a ferret, except this one was puke green. It was staring at Alan as if it expected an answer.

"Yes, but this is the first wooden one I have seen in Azor," answered Alan.

"It was dead when Azterl turned the trees to gold. All the dead trees resisted the spell."

"How is it that you can talk?"

"How is it you can talk, you little wise-ass jerk!"

Alan was shocked; he thought to himself, *It was odd enough to meet a talking animal, but a foul-mouthed one?*

"Who are you calling foul-mouthed, you slime-dripping scumbag?"

"Hey, you read my mind."

"That's right, jerk face. Now why don't you move on and let me do my job?"

"What is your job?"

"Oh crap, now you want to know my whole life story. You are a nosy son of an azdirktooth, aren't you? I am a spy for Azcob at the moment, but I will change sides if the pay is better."

Alan wondered what this creature sought as payment, then realized it could read his mind. He tried to wipe away the thought quickly, but was too late.

"I get paid money, of course. I suppose you'll want to know where I keep it hidden next. And quit calling me an animal in your little head. I am an *aztadzhick*. You really are a piss-complected moron, aren't you!"

Alan decided he had enough of this smart-mouthed aztadzhick, and he started down the path.

"Who are you calling a smart mouth, you yeast-infected, barf bag? Don't walk away from me, you simple-minded, piece-of-azdirktooth crap."

Alan's last thought was *I refuse to mentally spar with an unarmed aztadzhick.*

This only resulted in a continuous spiel of profanities from the aztadzhick, which lasted until Alan faded out of earshot. He was still not sure that wasn't a figment of his imagination, or a mirage, because of his thirst.

Why would anyone create such a vile little creature anyways? he thought.

The meadow turned into fields that were obviously tended. There were weird-looking crops growing on both sides of the path now. He went to one of the plants and pulled a tomato-sized piece of fruit off it. The fruit was orange with white strips. It had a thin skin, so he figured it didn't need to be peeled. He bit into it, noticing it tasted just like the juice both Azmora and Krhea had served him. He picked two more, eating them as he walked.

He came to the edge of a small village and decided since it was almost dark, he would wait a few more minutes before entering the town. Dusk fell to the pressing night as he entered the village. He kept to the shadows at first, but as he passed an inn, the shouting and sounds of happiness attracted him inside. He needed company for a little while, and hiding wasn't going to get him information.

There were about fifty people in the modest-sized establishment. They all crowded around a fighting ring, like the one in Krem's castle. There were two men in a heated fight in the ring. When one man knocked the other out, he exited the ring and was patted on the back by the spectators. The person behind the counter handed these same spectators wooden chips. Alan could only surmise this was what passed for money now; it made sense. The winner of the fight was handed a reward also.

He would need money while he was here in Azor, so he asked the man behind the counter if he could fight for pay also.

"Yeah, you can fight, but I won't pay you if you lose, and you'll owe me a night's work here in the inn and out in the *azdwark* stable."

"What will I get if I win?"

"I doubt you will, but I will pay you 10 percent of what I take in."

"It's a deal. When do I fight?"

"Right now, boy. Get in the ring, and whoever wishes to fight you will also enter the ring. Then there will be thirty seconds for bets to be placed with me. I then say fight, and you go at it until someone submits or is unconscious."

Alan stepped into the ring, and a man immediately stepped in across from him. Then the betting took place, and the innkeeper yelled, "Fight!"

His opponent was a big man, but still only about five feet tall. His face looked like someone beat him with an ugly stick. He was fast. He hit Alan before he could react, knocking him out of the ring. He landed flat on his back on the hard floor. A multitude of hands picked him up and shoved him back into the ring, laughing loudly.

Alan got his bearings and made like he was going to rush the man. The man planted his feet for the impact. But Alan jumped in the air and spun with a flying roundhouse kick to the man's head. Alan landed on his feet facing the man, but he was only stunned. The crowd was perfectly silent as if they had been the one who was kicked. Then the innkeeper let out a whoop and started clapping. The crowd was jarred out of their stupor and started clapping also.

AZOR'S REDEMPTION

Alan determined this guy wasn't going to submit. He looked even madder and uglier, if that was possible. Alan kicked the man in the solar plexus, and when he doubled over, Alan stepped in, grabbing him by the back of the head and shoved the guy's face into his up-thrusting knee. The man hit the floor and didn't move.

The crowd erupted in cheers and patted him on the back, even though all of them had bet against him. He made his way to the counter when some of Azcob's army came busting in the door.

"There he is! The lying aztadzhick told the truth for a change."

"You there, don't move. You're under arrest for homicide."

Just then, he felt a hand grab his shoulder and spin him around. It was the innkeeper. He shoved a handful of wooden coins into his hand and said, "The back door is that way. Hurry!"

Alan shoved the money into his pocket and ran for the back door.

As soon as he exited the door into the night's darkness, he felt three sets of hands grab him. He struggled, but he couldn't free himself from their grasp.

They were yelling, "Hurry, Azop, put a spell on him. He squirms like an *azvar*."

Alan heard a man say, "Are you sure it is him? This man has black hair, not yellow."

"He has black aztrin grease in his hair. It is all slimy. He also wears the color of Krem. I tell you he is the one."

"All right, I'll spell him. *Azregalin aztrebin*."

"It didn't work. He still fights us."

Alan felt someone knock two of the men off him; the other let go and backed away with his hands up. Alan realized who had knocked the men off of him; it was Lucky.

Lucky ran down the alley, and he followed him through the town and out the other side. They ran with Lucky leading. Then Lucky turned off the path and into the forest and stopped. Alan was glad he had stopped as he didn't think he could run any farther.

He hugged Lucky to him, "Thank you, Lucky, I am so glad to see you. I am sorry I left you behind. Azterl was right. I definitely needed you."

Alan thought of something else Azterl had said, "People's ideas and beliefs are hard to change, especially when they are presented with hard facts. Sometimes it is best not to even try."

He decided he wouldn't be attempting to convince the army of his mistake in killing their men. They had seen him help Kasan get free. They saw him flying with Kasan when he frightened their riding beasts. Now they saw him also wearing what they perceive as Krem's family color.

You couldn't get more hard facts than that, he thought. He would have to get to Azkrem and see the emperor while avoiding the army.

"Come on, my friend, we must cover as much ground as possible before daybreak." They continued on but traveled just inside the treeline, rather than in the open of the path itself, for about an hour. They were just about to return to the path to make better time when the army came riding by on their azdwarks. There were about thirty in all, and wizard Azop was traveling with them in his orange robe. Alan figured orange must be the color of Azterl's family, just as crimson was Krem's family color.

After the army had passed, he and Lucky returned to the path and seemed to make much better time. When the forest came to an end, Alan felt nervous about being out in the open, but there was nothing to be done about it. He noticed that the terrain was becoming more small hills than flat ground. The farther they traveled along, the steeper the path became, and he realized they were traveling up a mountain. He decided they must be above the thousand-foot point because for the first time, he actually felt a breeze. He had assumed that even on a mountain, the wind wouldn't be felt.

He thought, *Wouldn't the thousand-foot level fluctuate with the lay of the land? It seems not since the farther we go up, the stronger the breeze gets.*

There were only small shrubs growing along the path here and rocky cliffs on both sides as well. He decided they would have to find a safe place to stop pretty soon, a place where Lucky would be safe while he was gone. Sunrise was less than an hour away. Traveling was more difficult now, as they had to battle the wind and the incline.

A little while later, Lucky left the path off to the left and stopped a few yards away, then sat down facing Alan.

"What's up, Lucky? Is someone coming?" He just got up and moved another twenty yards farther and sat back down.

"All right, I will follow you if that's what you want. We need to find a place for you to hide anyways. It wouldn't be good for you to sit on the path for a day and night while I am gone."

When Alan caught up to Lucky, he got up, leading them to the cliffside. Then he turned back along the cliff in the opposite direction, to which they had been traveling.

"Lucky, this backtracking isn't going to get us to Azkrem. The sun will be up in half an hour, and I will have to leave."

Lucky continued along the cliffside, undaunted.

"Okay, I will continue to humor you a little farther."

They came to an outcropping of the cliff and had to go out and around it. When they got to the outer edge of it and started back in, he realized the outcropping concealed a cave opening.

Lucky walked into the cave, and Alan followed a few steps behind. As soon as he passed through the dark entrance, everything went black.

CHAPTER ELEVEN

When he again felt consciousness returning, a throbbing pain in the back of his head came with it. He came to the unmistakable conclusion that someone had busted him upside the head as he entered the cave entrance. He opened his eyes, and slowly, his surroundings came into focus. He was in a cave, or at least, part of a cave. It was more like a cave cell with nothing in it. There was an opening to the cell, the size of a regular doorway. He could hear voices coming from the other side of the doorway. He couldn't make out what they were saying. The cell, or cave walls, glowed just bright enough to see clearly. He tried to get up and go to the door when he realized he was bound. His feet were tied, as well as his hands. His head was pounding, making it difficult for him to think clearly.

Just then, he felt the world fall out from under him, and he was falling through the black nothingness, but he could still feel the bindings securely holding him. He finally felt the hardness of his prison bunk beneath him. He lay there waiting for the nausea to subside and then opened his eyes. His hands were tied behind his back, and his feet were tied together. He slid his arms down below his rear end and down his legs, then up over his feet and legs. With his hands in front of him now, he was able to manipulate the knots and get his hands free. He then untied his feet. Not wanting to explain the ropes, if they were found in his cell during a shakedown, he flushed them down the toilet.

"What the heck was that? Who hit me like that?" He thought miserably, *I hope Lucky got away, and he is all right. If anyone hurts him, they are going to pay. I wonder if it was Kasan again or Kalem or Krem or the army or another unknown enemy.*

AZOR'S REDEMPTION

He realized then that pretty much everyone on Azor was against him, or seemed to be.

"Sorry, Azterl, I just keep getting myself in one situation after another."

He thought about having to go back and face an unknown enemy. The advantage would be his because they wouldn't be expecting him to return. The only drawback would be some type of magic or force field on the doorway to the cell. He decided there was no sense in worrying about it now, plus his head was pounding.

He heard the guard coming down the tier, making his 6:00 a.m. count. "Can I get some Tylenol? I have a screaming headache."

"Put in a sick slip on the seven-to-three shift, and they'll get you some."

"Yeah, thanks for nothing."

Alan figured the guy probably got beat up for being miserable, and so they put him on the night shift. Most of the coward guards ended up on the night shift eventually. He figured if he lay down and tried to sleep, the pain may subside. He lay down, but sleep eluded him. He couldn't stop thinking about who hit him.

Finally, after eating breakfast, he was able to fall asleep. He woke up for lunch, feeling a little better, but his head was still quite tender to the touch.

"Kasan, if you did this, I am liable to kill you this time. I grow weary of your little tricks."

He again hoped Kasan hadn't hurt or caught Lucky. He had entered the cave just seconds before Alan had.

"Maybe Azterl's entry will give me some insight before I go back blindly into that situation." He went back to sleep, worrying about Lucky and what was to come.

He woke up at suppertime and sat on his bunk, then he thought to check his pockets, but nothing was there. Whoever knocked him out must have rifled through his pockets and took his money and the jar of grease. He puttered around the cell, trying to kill some time. Finally, nightfall came, and he lay down to read the entry, after covering his feet to hide his sneakers.

Entry 5

You should be well into your journey by now. Hopefully you are learning from your mistakes, as well as your successes. Your mission is no easy task, and it will take cunning and intelligence to accomplish saving the people. If you have moments of doubt, just remember the people cannot survive without your intervention.

  I have done all I could to assist you—both with this book and plans laid within Azor itself. It may be that my only creation, on my creation, could help save my creation. What you are looking for most may not be where you expect it, but you will understand what others can't. Don't overlook the obvious. I pray luck is with you throughout your travels.

  Before invoking the spell, he tried to come up with any hidden messages in the entry, but as usual, everything was far too vague. He invoked the spell and felt the now familiar feeling of the world falling away from him.

  When he landed, he wanted to open his eyes right away to be sure there was no one around. He needed the advantage of surprise on his side. When he was sure the nausea had passed, he opened his eyes. He was in the empty cave cell, but this time, he wasn't alone. Lucky sat on the floor across from him.

  "Well, I see they did get you after all. Don't worry, I'll get us out of here. Did they hurt you, buddy?" He started to get off the ground when he was completely shocked to hear Lucky speak to him.

  "Please stay seated for a few minutes." Lucky got up, but this time, he stood on two legs rather than four as Alan was used to seeing.

  "I must have hit my head again when I returned. This can't be happening."

  "I assure you it is real. I have been waiting for you to return, and I have a lot to tell you."

"But who hit me? Shouldn't we escape first? Are there guards?"

"Yes, there are guards, but they do not guard us."

"Then we can get out of here, and you can tell me how come you can talk now."

"Stay seated, Alan, and you will not be harmed!"

"Harmed, by who? There's no one here but you and me."

Alan realized there was something wrong here. Lucky seemed too in control to be a captive, and he had hidden the fact that he could talk.

"I was the one who knocked you out. It was necessary for me and my people's security. We couldn't allow you to see our hideout in case you escaped, as you are very good at."

"What is this all about? You knocked me out? Why?"

"I will explain if you just calm down and listen. You are not being held captive by anyone except me. I must warn you though, if you try to escape, I will kill you. Regrettably, I have to anyways if you aren't who we hope you are. I need you to read this to me. If you can do this, you will be safe."

Lucky tossed a rolled-up piece of aged paper on the floor where Alan sat. He hadn't even noticed Lucky had been holding it.

"I won't be threatened, Lucky, or whoever you are. I want some answers, and I want them now. How do I know you're not Kasan in disguise again?"

"Because I know you fooled Kasan with your fake "Hocus Pocus" spell when you really hid the jar of aztrin grease before you left me that morning. If I were Kasan, I wouldn't have known that. My real name is Azdebar, but I somewhat like Lucky, if you don't mind. I will answer any questions you wish, after you attempt to read that letter to me."

Alan felt betrayed by one of his two friends on Azor but decided he would do what he had to do. He unrolled the paper gently, as it was old, and he was afraid it would fall apart in his hands. Then he read aloud:

If you are able to read this, then I assume you are from earth, and you found my book and are now in the company of my good friend Azdebar. After reading this, make haste to my castle. There you will find a room with a bookshelf containing a collection of books I brought from earth with me. The book you want to find is called *The Pilgrim's Progress* by John Bunyan. In this book is a riddle that an educated eye will discover doesn't belong. The answer to this riddle, spoken aloud, as well as, the name of the recipient, spoken aloud, will result in them receiving my magic powers. If you have the wisdom to answer the riddle correctly, then I believe you will also have the wisdom to choose the right person. I said in my book that sending it away would cause my death. That was true but only because I had depleted myself by stashing the majority of my power away for the right person. I am sure Azdebar will show you the way to my castle, which was built for this reason, as well as others. Good luck in solving the riddle.

Sincerely,

Azterl

Alan rolled the paper back up and gave it back to Lucky. "Will you be traveling with me, Lucky?"

"I was hoping you would invite me to continue traveling with you. I will answer your questions now. I am glad you were able to read the writing as I have grown fond of you. It would have been terrible if I had to kill you."

"Why would you kill me?"

"You knew where we were, and the existence of Azor hinges on us completing our mission. Any threat to our survival, no matter how small, needs to be eliminated. There is no room for compassion."

"How come you never spoke to me before? It would have made things a lot easier."

"I was unable to talk to you. My people and I can only speak when we are on this mountain and then only when we are above the thousand-foot level."

"Why is that? Does it have something to do with the wind?"

"No, Azterl gave us this mountain as a refuge when Krem started killing us. He would have wiped us out completely, but we were Azterl's creation, so he made sure we survived."

Alan remembered Azterl's entry saying, "My only creation, on my creation, could help save my creation." He knew now that Azterl was referring to—the azkibitz.

He asked Lucky, "What can you do to save Azor?"

"We have held this post for years awaiting your arrival. Now it is up to you. We are here at your disposal."

"I am still confused."

"Let me tell you the story and help ease your confusion. When Krem started killing the azkibitz to punish Azterl for the accident that caused Rhea's death, he trained the azreyvicks to help hunt us. Over time, the azreyvicks started hunting and killing us on their own. They would take the dead bodies to Krem, and he would hang the hides in his fighting room. Azterl, in his efforts to save us, built this cave with his magic. The azreyvicks do not come here. They have serious difficulty flying in the wind. They always fly beneath the thousand-foot level, and this keeps them off our mountain. One day, Azterl came to visit us and cast a spell allowing us to speak, but only when we are on the mountain."

"Why just here?"

"You are the reason for that. We were charged with securing his message until it could be delivered."

"I suspect that Emperor Azcob is also from earth, so why not give the message to him?"

"Everything is tied together and all part of Azterl's plan. There were crucial reasons for us not to be able to talk when off the mountain. We were not allowed to give the message to anyone, except a stranger to Azor. The stranger had to come to the mountain of their own accord, as you did. Azterl was also concerned that, if one of our number was captured and tortured, they may reveal our location. He told us that only one other person in Azor could read this message besides him, and that was the wizard Krem. He was a powerful wizard, and his powers falling into the wrong hands would be very dangerous."

"What about Azcob?"

"If he is from earth as you suspect, then he probably could have read the message, but he never came to the mountain, to our disappointment. When you went away with Kasan, I was sure you were never going to come here either. Do you remember the day I tried to get you to go down the road to the left, which would have brought you here?"

"Yeah, I remember, but I went to the right and ended up at Azmora's cottage."

"I was only able to suggest the left path because you asked. If you hadn't have asked, then I wouldn't have been able to interfere in your decision. Azterl felt really strong about people having the freedom to choose."

"Yes, he would. If I guess right, Krem and he left earth back in 1690. This was a time on earth when the people were hanging and burning witches."

"What is a witch, and why were they being hung and burned?"

"A witch is someone who practiced magic. They were hung and burned because of the differences in their practices and beliefs compared to others."

"Come on with me. I'll introduce you to the rest of my people and my family. Then we will eat and be on our way to Azterl's castle, if that's okay with you."

"Yes, that sounds like a plan, but I don't look forward to trying to figure out who should get Azterl's magic. That's if I can even come up with the answer to the riddle."

He followed Lucky, or Azdebar, out of the cell, still having a hard time getting used to the way he now walked.

The room they walked through was a huge cave. There were azkibitz of all ages running around. They were all busy doing something; it was like a beehive of activity. Some carried around food. The children ran around playing a type of tag game, and couples walked around hand in hand. There wasn't a difference between the sexes that was visible other than the female's ears lay closer to their heads.

There were hundreds of doorways in the walls of the cave. As they walked along, the azkibitz looked on in surprise and pleasure. Lucky led him through one of the doorways.

"They know you are the one we have waited for so long to arrive. Ever since Azterl came to us with his message, we have talked of the day when the stranger would come. When things would again be put right, and we could roam freely as we once did."

The room they entered resembled a one-room apartment. There was furniture, only larger than normal to accommodate their size. A female tended to a cub in the corner of the room.

Lucky introduced them, "This is my mate, Azhegal and my daughter, Azhoopo."

"Nice to meet the family of such a brave azkibitz." Alan gestured.

"Azdebar tells us that you saved him from Kasan. You must be the earth stranger we have waited for. I thank you for saving my mate."

"You are welcome, but Azdebar saved my life numerous times—from poison and from soldiers. You truly should be proud of him."

"Why would the soldiers try to capture you? Aren't you on the same side?"

"They did not know who he was. Now get us some food and drink please. We must leave soon for Azing."

After they ate and drank their fill, Lucky gave Alan back his aztrin grease jar and the wooden coins. "You will need this to hide your yellow hair, and we may need the coins to bribe the *azvars* that guard Azterl's castle."

"What is an azvar? The army soldiers who held me at the back door of the inn said I squirm like one."

"I can't really describe them so well. You will see for yourself soon enough."

Lucky led Alan back out into the crowded main cave. They approached another doorway. This one actually had a door on it, but no handle. As they stood in front of the door, other azkibitz started gathering around.

"In the name of Azterl, I bring the stranger from earth!" Lucky stated in a loud voice.

The door disappeared, to the delight of the crowd. They cheered and patted him on the back, yelling, "Well wishes to the stranger."

Alan followed Lucky through the doorway. As soon as they stepped through, the door reappeared behind them, blocking the view and noise of the crowd.

They now stood in a tunnel that slanted downward. The walls glowed as they had in the main cave.

"This is a passageway that Azterl built to take us quickly to his castle when you arrived. It has never been used, as Azterl sealed the door magically. Only I knew the spell to open it. The spell would be passed down to my offspring had you not come before I died."

"But your cub, Azhoopo, is so young. What if you had died before having her?"

"She is my thirty-seventh cub. The oldest would have received the spell to open the door."

They walked on in silence for some time. The tunnel leveled off eventually, and Lucky dropped down on all four feet and walked along. Alan thought he did it out of habit, but when he tried to talk to Lucky, he realized why he no longer walked on two feet.

"How long will it take us to get to Azterl's castle?"

Lucky only looked back at him over his shoulder and continued on.

"We must have left the mountain back there when you stopped walking upright, huh?"

He received no answer and decided he was right. Lucky couldn't talk anymore, so he walked on in silence.

The tunnel ended abruptly at a wall that blended into the sides of the cave. Alan thought to ask Lucky for advice, then remembered he would get no answer. He leaned against the wall to think about the situation, and the wall moved inward from his weight. They stepped through into a hallway of what Alan figured must be the castle. Lucky went to the left, and Alan followed him. The wall moved back into place, and Alan couldn't see any evidence of the opening from this side. They walked down the hall past many doors and came to a stairwell leading up. At the top of the stairway, Lucky stopped, causing Alan to bump into him.

"What's wrong, Lucky?" Alan looked down the new hallway they had entered but saw nothing. "Come on, there is no one here." Alan passed Lucky and took a few steps down the hallway when he ran into something about knee high. He would have fallen on his face if he didn't put his hands out to catch himself. He looked but couldn't see anything that would trip him. He heard a sound like many suction cups being stuck and unstuck from the floor, but still couldn't see anything causing it. Then he thought he saw a movement—but nothing was there. The sucking sounds continued and stopped right in front of him. He reached out and touched something but couldn't see what he touched. He ran his hand along whatever it was he felt. It was about three feet long, with five legs on each side, and about a foot and a half high. Its feet were shaped like a bell, which must account for the suction sounds they made. He got to his feet and tried to go around what he felt. It moved to block his way.

"What are you? What do you want?" Alan looked at Lucky, but he only sat on the floor, waiting.

"You must be an azvar, and you're protecting the castle. Well, Lucky told me I may have to bribe you."

He reached into his pocket and took out a couple of coins and held them out. Nothing happened. He tossed them on the floor where he had felt the azvar standing. The sucking sounds began again, then the coins disappeared. The sounds moved off down the hallway until they faded to nothing.

"Come on, Lucky, before it returns for more money."

Lucky got up and walked down the hall, passing nine doors, then he stopped in front of one. Alan tried the door, and it opened. They stepped in, and Alan thought he had stepped back in time. It was like a museum emulating the early pilgrim life. The furniture was crude wooden artifacts. There was a table, some chairs, and a spinning wheel in one corner. The shelves contained clay crockery and wooden utensils. There was a fireplace with a black iron pot hanging in it.

"This room's items were definitely brought from early New England," Alan guessed.

In one corner was a chair and bookshelf. He walked toward it, looking for the book *The Pilgrim's Progress*. There were only six books on the shelf, and none of them were the right one. He could see the thick dust on everything except a spot that appeared to have been occupied by five or so books. The clean area had just recently been made, as the dust coat was extremely light.

"Oh no, someone took the book! It held the riddle to all of Azterl's powers. Now someone has it. But who?"

CHAPTER TWELVE

As Alan stood there staring at the empty space on the shelf, he remembered something Azterl had said in his last entry, "What you are looking for most may not be where you expect it to be, but only you can understand it."

Alan thought he must have been talking about the book not being where I would expect it to be, but he was wrong about me being the only one who could understand it. Both Krem and Emperor Azcob could read it and maybe one of them had it.

Then he remembered Azterl went on to say, "Only if you are from my homeland can you read the meaning in my carefully laid plans for assisting Azor." That could mean that whoever has the book won't understand the meaning of a riddle in the book unless they are actually looking for it.

"Well, Lucky, let's hope that is the case. We must get to Azkrem and find out if Emperor Azcob has the book we need." They left the room and entered the hallway again, running right into someone, and it wasn't an azvar this time.

"What are you doing in my father's study?" said the woman standing there in an orange robe.

"We don't mean any harm. I was just looking for a book to read."

"You couldn't read any of those books. Only my father and Krem understand them. Now tell me the truth. You wear the color of Krem, but I have never seen you before. Are you another of Krem's bastard children?"

"I am no friend or relative of Krem. I am a friend of your father."

"You lie again! I know my father's friends, and you are not one of them. It would be hard to miss someone of your height and blue eyes. Wait—you are the murderer of Azcob's soldiers! You say you are no friend of Krem, yet you helped Kasan escape and chased the soldier's azdwarks away. You are a friend and companion of an azkibitz though, which doesn't figure. My brother Azop tells me he was unable to put a spell on you, so you must be a wizard. There are only two families of wizards in Azor, and you are not from my family. You look like Azcob in a way. Nothing about you I can understand, so you will accompany me to Azkrem to see Emperor Azcob, and he can decide what to do with you."

"We had just decided that Azkrem was to be our destination, so if you wish to accompany us, then you may."

"I'm supposed to trust you to turn yourself in to the emperor with the charges you are accused of?"

"You don't have much choice. I have no reason to lie to you. I am trying to help the people of Azor, and whether you can believe me or not doesn't matter. I proved to your brother that his magic couldn't affect me, so you have no way of forcing me to go anywhere." Alan was sure that Krhea's protection spell had worn off by now, but he hoped his bluff would hold.

"All right, I don't trust you, but we will travel to Azkrem together. Can you bring your friend the azkibitz magically?"

"No. My power is strong enough, but I have never been to Azkrem, and without knowing my destination, I cannot travel safely with magic," Alan bluffed again.

"We shall use my azdwarks then. What is your name?"

Alan decided to use the name Azmora and he had come up with. "My name is Azearth, and my friend's name is Lucky. I assume you are Aztrion, right?"

"Yes, I am Aztrion. You have a name that shows loyalty to my father. You are a difficult person to figure out."

"If you don't mind, I am in a hurry to meet with the emperor. If we could leave now, we could get there that much sooner."

"How did you get past the azvar that guards here?"

"I used magic to get by it."

"But magic is useless against the azvar. That is why they were created as castle guardians."

"My magic is not the same as yours or anyone's on Azor."

"Yes, your magic must be powerful. Come, I am sure Azcob would like very much to talk to you."

The three of them left the castle and found the two azdwarks waiting in the stables. Once they were saddled, Alan got his first experience of riding one of the strange beasts. It was a little rough of a ride, but the azdwark covered a lot of ground quickly. Lucky ran alongside them, and Alan was surprised that Lucky never tired or fell behind. They rode on nonstop until nightfall and came to a village Aztrion called Azon.

"We will stop here and get something to eat and drink if you don't mind."

Alan didn't mind at all. He was more than happy to get off the azdwark for a little while.

"How much farther is it to Azkrem?"

"About double the distance we have today traveled. There is one more village halfway between here and Azkrem that is called Azif. We will travel around it as the people are now loyal to Krem. He destroyed their crops, blackmailing them through hunger to serve his cause. Hunger can change a person's loyalty pretty quickly. He told the people that my father didn't care about them and that's why he left them to fend for themselves. The people couldn't deny my father's disappearance, so they turned their loyalty to Krem."

Alan realized that Aztrion also believed that Azterl had just gone into hiding. He decided to keep his agreement with Azmora and not speak of Azterl's death.

They approached an inn, and Aztrion indicated that this was where they would eat. As they entered, Alan saw that there was a fighting ring in the center of the room. It was set up exactly as the one he had fought in at the Azden inn. There weren't any fights taking place yet, maybe it was too early in the day. There were actually only a dozen men in the whole establishment. They took a seat by the front door at a small table. Lucky sat at Alan's feet.

A tiny older woman came over to them and asked what they would like. Alan let Aztrion order for both of them and Lucky. While they sat quietly waiting for their food to come, a few dozen people drifted in, and the inn started to come alive. By the time their food and drinks were actually set in front of them, there was a fight getting set up in the ring. Alan and Aztrion watched with interest as the fighters locked in battle. It seemed to Alan that the style of fighting here was predominantly wrestling. It was an effective way to fight, but it was also time- and energy-consuming.

Alan noticed that Aztrion was staring at him as he watched the fight. "What is it that makes you stare like that?"

"I am sorry, Azearth. I was just thinking about you beating Azire. He is the best fighter in Azor. You must have caught him sleeping. Yet he tells the story as if you fairly beat him."

"I am glad to hear he is honorable, but I did kind of catch him when he was off guard. He was surprised at my fighting style, and it provided me the opportunity to strike a knockout blow."

"Why did you not kill him as you did the other two soldiers that you fought?"

"It wasn't my intention to kill anyone. I was outnumbered and didn't know their intentions."

"If you are a friend of my father and your loyalties lay with him as your name suggests, then why help Kasan escape?"

"Kasan tricked me with his magic into thinking he was a helpless female. Since I came here to help the people of Azor hold on to their freedom, I helped."

"Surely Kasan couldn't trick a wizard with your great power."

Alan was contemplating how to respond to that without revealing his bluff when two drunk men approached their table.

"Hello, brother, could we assist you with this fine-looking lady?" said the uglier of the two.

"I am not your brother, and I wouldn't disrespect the lady if I were you."

"You wear the color of our boss. Are you not here to help us capture her?"

Alan started to get out of his seat to confront the drunk, but was hit on the back of his head. He saw stars and felt his knees give way as darkness overtook his mind.

The next time he regained consciousness, he was bound and gagged with some nasty-tasting stuff in his mouth preventing him from speaking. He was in a box about six by six that he was sure was a cage wagon of some sort. He could hear the squeaking of the wheels as the wagon bumped along the rough path.

He immediately wondered what happened to Aztrion and Lucky and assumed they had been captured as well. He remembered the men saying he was wearing the color of their boss, so they were obviously working for Krem. I imagined they were taking me to Kreal, which means it was going to be a long trip, and I would be able to escape when I get pulled back to earth. I would return back to wherever I leave from, but that could put me two days behind Aztrion and Lucky. I thought they could make it to Kreal in two days, but probably not at this slow-plodding pace. He got up on his knees and attempted to peek out the back doors of the wagon. The space was too tiny to see anything but darkness. If we were still heading north, then we might stop in Azif. Aztrion said it was the next town, but the people of Azif were loyal to Krem, so most likely we would stop. We would probably go around Azkrem on our way to Kreal, which was far north. Krem would no doubt use Aztrion to blackmail Emperor Azcob and her brother Azop into giving up. I really must find the book straight away, or Krem was going to succeed in destroying Azor. When I do find it, who the heck was I going to give Azterl's powers to? Also, I don't even know if I can figure out the riddle. I just have to somehow help Aztrion and Lucky escape before they arrive in Kreal.

Alan lay back onto the floor of the wagon and dozed off with the rhythmic bumping and swaying of the ride. When he opened his eyes again, nothing had changed. The wagon still rolled on steadily. While he sat there thinking about his situation, the world fell out from under him, and he felt the now familiar black nothingness surround him.

*****

He felt the uncomfortable hardness of his cell bunk beneath him, as he lay there with his eyes closed for quite some time. Even after the spinning had ended, he lay there. He tried blocking everything about Azor out of his mind, but his efforts proved fruitless. The problems he faced in Azor kept creeping to the surface. Finally, he opened his eyes and sat up on his bunk. He decided he needed a nice hot cup of coffee. As he got up to make his coffee, he realized that he still had the jar of black Aztrin grease in his pocket. He also found the eleven wooden coins he had won while fighting in Azden. He looked at the coins closely for the first time. They were the size of silver dollars, but they showed no monetary worth printed on them. On one side was an old dead tree that looked just like the only real tree left on Azor, and the other side pictured a tiny map. He wondered if this was a map of Azor. There were no names, only dots where villages would be and a tiny star in the center, with four roads shooting off the star, in the four directions, and all the dots were along these roads. Azkrem is the capital of Azor, so that must be represented by the star.

Aztrion told me there were two towns between Azkrem and Azing, and there were only three dots to the south on the coins. I guess that meant Azing was the farthest town south. I came from the east, and I saw the fork in the road here, so following this road back toward the west, this dot should be Azden where I fought in the ring. That meant I was only one town away from Azkrem when Lucky knocked me out. I supposed that was necessary since I found out so much from him.

Alan heard the guard coming down the tier doing his six-thirty count, so he lay back like he was asleep until he passed. He decided he better hide the money and jar of black aztrin grease. Then he realized he still had the grease in his hair, so he washed it out as best he could with the trickle of water coming from his sink. He hid the coins in an empty milk carton in his trash and hid the jar behind his shampoo and conditioner on the shelf. He hoped that if his cell got shaken down, they would miss the jar.

He ate breakfast when it was brought around and went to sleep with a troubled and heavy mind. He was awakened after just two and a half hours of sleep by the guard banging on the bars of his cell door.

"Hey, Eliot, the DSU Review Board wants to see you."

"I just saw the DSU Board a few months ago, what do they want?"

"I don't know, I am not a mind reader. Do you want to see them or not?"

"Yeah, give me a few minutes to brush my teeth and wash up."

"You got five minutes, and I will be back."

Alan checked his cell to make sure everything looked in order in case the guard checked the cell out while he was gone, then he got ready.

"All right, Eliot, back up to the bars to get cuffed and shackled."

The guard escorted Alan to the hearing room where the chairman of the board spoke to him.

Mr. Eliot, we have looked over your record. You were housed in the Awaiting Action Unit for ten months with no disciplinary infractions. We gave you two years DSU for your last bit of trouble, but we are prepared to send you to Nine Block today. You will stay there for two months barring any incidents, and then we will send you to the Phase Two Program at Norfolk. If you can follow the program rules there, you can be back in a medium-security population in six months' time. The choice is yours. Your behavior will show us if you really deserve to be out of twenty-four-hour lockup."

"Can't I stay here in Ten Block for the two months and then transfer to Phase Two from here?"

Alan was thinking about the few days that would pass before his property would catch up to him in Nine Block, and he had to get back to Azor.

"You know that Nine Block is the next level toward Phase Two, and we don't think it is in your best interest to skip that step."

"If I refuse to go to Nine Block, then the whole deal is off, huh?"

"Yes, that is the way it is!"

"Could I have permission to bring a book with me to Nine Block?"

"We have nothing to do with the property department. Do you wish to go along with our recommendation, or not?"

Alan thought about it for a minute. He decided that Azor would have to get along without him for a few days. He needed this chance to get out of lockdown and back in population.

"Yes, I will agree to your offer."

"Good luck, Mr. Eliot. Your behavior will decide whether everything goes as we discussed here today."

Alan went back to his cell and packed his small number of belongings for the second time in less than a week. Once again, he thought it couldn't hurt to ask if he could carry the book with him, but the guard denied his request.

When he got to Nine Block, he settled in and waited for property to get his belongings back to him. The difference between Nine Block and Ten Block was not significant. You were at least able to go outside in a fenced-in area the size of half a basketball court, along with the other prisoners on your tier. You were allowed out three times a week, for two hours at a time. There was a basketball hoop inside the fence, but most times, the ball was popped as soon as it hit the razor wire along the fence. It would take about a week to get a new one each time. The guys would run laps around the area and do calisthenics to keep themselves active.

It took twenty-one days for property to get him his stuff this time. Regardless of how many letters he wrote to them to complain, it did no good. It was a very long and stressful three weeks in which he imagined a million scenarios of what was possibly happening in Azor.

As he lay down to read Azterl's entry that evening, he wished he still had the coins and Aztrin grease to take back with him. It would be tougher traveling with his blond hair and having no money. He looked around his cell for something to bring with him for this trip. He couldn't decide on anything, so he grabbed a photo of a beautiful sunset. As he stuck it in his pocket, he thought it was a silly idea, but he was in a hurry.

He settled down and anxiously read Azterl's next entry.

Entry 6

I have talked the last few times about the failures of Krem and myself, but I don't regret everything. I still think Azor is a good idea. We had our homeland's experience to learn from, which gave us an advantage. There is a popular saying where I am from, "If I only knew then, what I know now." This is a true statement, and we did know a lot when we created Azor, but there is so much that we could have done better. The one thing we did was eliminate weaponry, or better yet, didn't introduce it into Azor in the first place. We made fighting a sport rather than an act of violence. Teaching everyone a new language was beyond our magic, so we continued speaking our native tongue but called it Azorian.

We were able, through much effort, to take away people's ability to read and write in our native tongue. Eventually, out of necessity, a new written language was developed. Our reason for eliminating the old way of reading was to make sure Azor wasn't corrupted by any writings, or even the few books Krem and I brought in. This was a censoring of sorts, but we believed it necessary to the success of our vision. The books I brought over were reminders for me of what I didn't want Azor to become.

Take what's left when facing the rising sun with doubts. You still won't be satisfied, but at least, you won't search in vain the same place again. Your likeness will be what will save you in times of trouble. Once again, be careful in your travels.

Alan was so anxious to get back to Azor that he didn't even give any thought to his trip. He just invoked Azterl's spell.

*****

He felt the world fall out from under him and realized it didn't matter if you were ready or not for the fall through the nothingness, it sucked either way. When he stopped falling, he didn't feel the familiar ground beneath him. All of a sudden he fell again, about two feet and hit the ground. Like an idiot, he opened his eyes, as he was startled by this unusual occurrence. The spinning made him feel like throwing up. He lay there holding on to the ground for some time. He realized that when he last left Azor, he was in the wagon, which must have been about two feet off the ground in this spot. So he returned to that spot and fell to the ground. In his excitement to get here, he hadn't thought it through. When his stomach settled down, he opened his eyes to find that he most assuredly was on the dirt road, surrounded by trees on both sides.

He wondered aloud, "Which way should I go? Did we pass Azkrem while I was in the wagon? If I go back south and we didn't pass Azkrem yet, I'll end up in Azif. That will be a waste of time. If I go north and we already passed Azkrem, it could be rough going for me as I appear now. What did Azterl's entry say?"

"Take what's left when facing the rising sun with doubts."

"I hope this is the right definition to his vague hints. Left when facing the rising sun would lead me north. Which would suggest we hadn't yet passed Azkrem. I wonder if we have passed Azif. I guess I'll find out soon enough."

Alan walked north along the dirt road for quite some time. The sun was straight overhead when he finally saw a village in the distance. There had been swamp water on both sides of the road for some time now. He had no choice except to go right into the city, or go all the way back and try to go around the swamp and village. It was too far to go back, so he decided to take a chance and enter the village, hoping it wasn't Azif.

CHAPTER THIRTEEN

Alan approached the village with caution; he wished it were evening instead of the break of day. The forest and swamps ended meeting fields full of crops. There were cottages on each farming lot. As Alan walked along the path, people were coming out of their cottages to begin work in the fields. Luckily, most were too busy to even notice him as he walked toward what now appeared to be a city rather than a village. The road he was on led directly down the center of the city. There were stores and houses on both sides of the street for as far as he could see. There were side streets shooting off the main road, but they all went very short distances before ending.

The road that he walked on was coming alive with people as they started their business of the day. Shopkeepers opened their doors and pulled carts, as well as led azdwarks in front of larger wagons. He received looks of confusion as he walked along, making him a little nervous. He wondered if this was Azif or Azkrem. He approached a man up ahead setting up his shop area with all types of fruit.

Alan asked him, "Excuse me, sir, could you tell me the name of your city?"

The man turned around and stared at Alan, then walked into his shop and closed the door.

"Not very friendly here I guess."

Just then, Alan caught a reflection of himself in a piece of shiny metal hanging on one of the buildings. He realized his height, blond hair, and blue eyes must seem like quite a sight to these people. He decided to just move on quietly and see if he could find anything that resembled a castle before the city ended. He was sure that was where he would find Emperor Azcob, if this was Azkrem.

All of a sudden there was a huge man standing in his path. He was wearing tan baggy-type pants and light leather shoes, as well as a harness. This leather harness started on one hip and ran up and over the opposite shoulder and back down to the same hip.

"I am Azire. I requested that I be permitted to greet you by myself and bring you in. Will you come with me peacefully?"

"So you're Azire. I figured we would meet up again. Where would you like me to accompany you to?"

"To see the elders, where you will be formally read the charges against you."

"If I do not wish to be taken as a prisoner to these people?"

"Then I will be forced to attempt bringing you in by force, but either way, you won't make it out of Azkrem without answering to the charges. We have known you were here since you passed into the most outer limits of our city. We let you get this far, assuring escape is impossible."

"I wish to speak to Azcob the emperor. Will he be present at this elders meeting?"

"No, but you will be brought before him for his decision on your punishment."

"I will go with you, but not as your prisoner."

"I am fine with that, as I hoped we wouldn't have to fight again. I am not afraid of you. I just would prefer not taking the chance of being defeated in the street in front of all these people. I have had a more difficult time doing my duty since our last encounter. People jest, behind my back of course, because I was bested by you. They say I allowed two of my men to die and then ran. I assure you I didn't run out of fear. I felt that warning the emperor was more important than saving face."

"I believe that, Azire, as I have heard you were the number one fighter on Azor. I also don't wish to fight you again without the element of surprise I had last time. Shall we go see the elders now?"

They continued down the road together, receiving even more glances than Alan had received alone. Each side street they passed produced a couple more soldiers, which fell in line marching a distance behind them. Like it or not, Alan realized he was a prisoner after all. Finally, they stopped in front of a large stone building, where two soldiers were stationed.

"You will go with these men to face the elders. May Azterl be with you."

"Aren't you going to come with us?"

"No, I have duties to see to, but I will see you again soon."

"I am sorry about your men, Azire."

"Yes, for some reason, I believe you are."

Alan was escorted into the building by the two soldiers and led down the hallway to a bench.

"We will wait here until we are summoned!"

Alan sat down, and the soldiers sat on either side of him. After an hour, Alan asked what the held up was, but the soldiers acted as if they didn't hear him. He stood up; they stood up. He sat down; they sat down. He stood up and took a couple steps as if leaving. This got a reaction. The soldiers blocked his path, saying, "You must wait until we are summoned!"

He was about to protest when a door opened up farther down the hall, and a little old man came out.

"You may bring the prisoner in now."

The soldiers escorted him into the room. There were seven old men seated in a semicircle facing where Alan and the soldiers stood.

The man in the middle, who appeared to be older than the rest, if that was possible said, "We are the elders of Azor. You are the accused. You are charged with two counts of murder of soldiers in the emperor's army. You are further charged with scattering azdwarks that are also in the emperor's army, causing the death of one, as it ran frightened. How do you wish to be put to death?"

"Put to death! I don't get to defend myself? What is this? I don't get to see the emperor or face my accusers?"

"We are your accusers, and we need not bother the emperor with such a cut-and-dried case as this. He has other more serious things to deal with. If you have no preference as to the style of your death, then I sentence you to fight other prisoners also sentenced to death, until which time you die."

"What if I win?"

"You will fight over and over until you eventually die."

"I demand to see the emperor!"

"A condemned man demands nothing. We hear only a ghost talking. Guards, remove this corpse from our chambers!"

Alan turned to fight but was grabbed by both soldiers and wrestled from the room where more soldiers waited to help drag him down a flight of stairs at the end of the hall. The stairs led down to the dungeon. Lining both sides of the hall were cell doors made of iron. As they marched him down the hallway, he could see that there were about ten other prisoners and two empty cells. These other prisoners were some of the biggest and ugliest men Alan had yet seen on Azor. He was led into a cell, and the guards put a shackle around his leg. The shackle was connected to a four-foot long heavy chain that was connected to a bracket on the wall.

"You can't do this. I have to see the emperor!"

"Listen to him," the guards joked with one another. "When we have lunch with the emperor, we'll tell him, hahaha."

"Okay then, when do I fight?"

"He is anxious to die. You will fight first, today at noon, since you're in such a hurry."

The guards walked out, laughing as they locked the door and left.

Alan stood there wondering how he once again found himself locked in a cell. Finally, he just sat down on the floor and contemplated how he was going to get out of this one. A tray was suddenly slid under the bars of the door.

"You made it just in time for breakfast." It was a teenage boy who slid the food to him.

"Wait, let me talk to you for a minute."

"I am not supposed to talk to the prisoners, but the guards are eating also, so be quiet and quick."

"Can you get a message to the emperor for me? It is very important!"

"I have many chores to do at my father's inn. I must deliver the food my father is obligated to provide to the jail for a year. It was his punishment from the elders. This only adds to my long list of chores, and I can't do anything until I'm finished."

"If you bring my message to the emperor, he will be grateful and may even suspend your father's punishment. This would make your chores lighter, right?"

"Give me the message, and I will see what I can do after I am done here."

"Tell the emperor that his brother from earth is being held prisoner here in the dungeon. You got it?"

"Yes, his brother from earth."

Alan was also going to tell him he was fighting to the death at noon, so hurry, but the boy was gone. He ate a piece of the fruit from the tray, not out of hunger, but for lack of anything else to do. Hours passed with no sign that his message was delivered. He wondered if the emperor would even come if he received his message. He figured he would have to come just out of curiosity that someone from earth was here.

As he was thinking this, he heard noise outside his cell, then the door was opened. Two guards came in and removed the shackle from his leg.

"You have been summoned to appear, come along now."

The soldiers escorted him out of the cell and down the hall past the other cells. They went up the stairs, but when they reached the stairs, they went the opposite way from before when he saw the elders. They came to a huge open door at the end of the hall, and he was shoved through the door, and it was shut behind him. He was now standing in a huge room with a balcony running the full length of the room.

Standing directly across from him was a man that stood about five feet tall, but was at least that wide across and all muscle.

"Wait a minute! You said I was summoned to appear, I thought—"

"You thought what?" said one of the guards from up in the balcony. "Did you think it was the emperor who summoned you? Hahaha!"

The soldier continued, "The boy you gave your message to is the kid brother of one of the soldiers you killed."

"What? Are you kidding me?"

"We were actually concerned he may poison you before you were able to fight. We don't want anything like that to ruin our entertainment. Now you will fight to the death. Kegin is your fellow prisoner. He knows the routine. He has killed his last twenty-seven opponents and has lived to fight another day because of it. Now let's see some of this fancy fighting Azire speaks of."

Alan had his back to Kegin, as he was looking up at the soldier in the balcony. Without warning, he felt the air rush out of his lungs as he was grabbed from behind in a bear hug. His arms were pinned to his sides, and he was being squeezed so tightly that he couldn't catch his breath. He started to get dizzy and felt his grasp on consciousness slipping.

"Haha, just as I thought, Azire made up the story of your outrageous fighting talent to cover his cowardice of running away from you," said the guard from the balcony.

"You will get a chance to find out" came a voice from behind the guard. "But for now, you will stop this fight. I have come from the emperor, and he wishes to speak to this man."

"The fight cannot be stopped, Azire. You know Kegin is sentenced to death and won't stop if ordered, especially now that he knows the emperor himself wants to see this prisoner."

Alan was just starting to black out when he saw Azire jump down into the ring and run toward them. Kegin pushed Alan away from him and prepared himself for Azire's charge. Alan lay there gulping in deep breaths of air, trying to ward off the still sinking blackness of unconsciousness trying to overtake him.

Kegin and Azire locked together in battle, both men trying to gain the advantage. All of a sudden, Azire lost his footing for just a moment, and Kegin got him in a bear hug. They were chest to chest, but Azire's arms were free, so he attempted to choke Kegin. This effort was fruitless, as Kegin just flexed his neck, thwarting Azire's attempt.

Alan could see Azire's strength ebbing away, as his had moments ago.

"Azire, cup your hands and clap them together hard on his ears!" yelled Alan.

Azire clumsily did as Alan suggested, and Kegin let out a tremendous howl of pain. He let go of Azire, brought his hands up to his ears while dropping to his knees, and then fell on his face to the ground. He lay on the ground holding his ears and whimpering like a baby.

Azire walked over to Alan and helped him up, saying, "Thanks, but what did I do to him?"

"You popped his eardrums. He will live, but I doubt he will hear so well."

"Open the door and put Kegin back in his cell. This man is coming with me. I will be sure to come back and give you a chance to find out how much of a coward I am!"

The door was opened immediately, and Alan and Azire exited the ring, leaving Kegin whimpering on the floor.

Together, they walked out of the stone building and down the street.

"Thank you for saving me back there, Azire."

"How did he get such a fighter as yourself into a position like that anyways?"

"He grabbed me from behind as I talked to the guard."

"Yes, I believe that. He was sent by Krem to capture Azonia."

"Who is Azonia?"

"She is the daughter of Emperor Azcob and Empress Azonian."

They stopped in front of a small indistinct cottage that looked just like all the others on the street.

"We are here!"

"I thought we were going to see the emperor?"

"This is the emperor's cottage. Come on now, he will be wondering what took so long to retrieve you. He seemed anxious to talk to you."

"Not as anxious as I am to talk to him."

They went up to the door, and Azire knocked. The door opened immediately, and a woman of about eighteen stood there in the entrance.

"We have come to see your father. I bring—what is your name anyway?"

Azire turned toward Alan when he didn't answer. Alan was staring at the woman standing in the doorway.

"Are you sure you didn't hit your head while you were fighting Kegin?" Azire teased Alan.

"What? Oh no, I am sorry! What did you say?"

"What is your name?"

"Azearth," he said, more to her than Azire.

"Well, this is Azonia."

"I d-d-don't know w-w-what you're talking about," Elsa stuttered.

"Likewise. Come in, my father waits for you in his office."

They went into the living room, and Alan didn't once take his eyes off Azonia. She led them down a short hall and knocked on the door they stopped in front of.

"Father, it is Azire and a man called Azearth, here to see you."

"Come in," said a voice from beyond the door.

Azonia opened the door and waved them in.

"Please bring our guests some refreshments, Azonia," said the man seated behind the desk.

He appeared to be in his midfifties, with brown sandy hair and brown eyes. He stood and reached over his desk with his hand out. Alan shook his hand.

"My name is Azcob. I am sorry for any mishandling by the elders. They mean well and try to deal with as much on their own without bothering me."

"I am Azearth, and I am no worse for wear thanks to Azire."

"Azearth, huh? Azcob looked at Alan with a knowing smile. "Be seated, gentlemen."

"Excuse me, sir. I would like to attend to something at the hall of elders if I am not needed here."

"No, you are not really needed, but you may stay, Azire."

"I would prefer to go attend to this, sir."

"You are free to go. Thank you for escorting Azearth to me safely and please return when you have completed your business. Azonian expects you for dinner tonight, and you wouldn't want to upset the empress."

"No, sir, I wouldn't. I will be back by dinner."

"Good luck, Azire," said Alan with a wink. He knew exactly what business Azire was off to attend to, and he didn't feel the least bit sorry for the guard at Elders Hall.

When Azcob and Alan were alone, Azcob spoke first.

"I assumed you were from earth considering the description that Azire first brought me months ago. Obviously, the name you chose says it all. What is your real name?"

"Alan Eliot, sir."

"How is it that you came to have Azterl's book?"

"Your daughter donated it to the prison library where I am serving time."

"How do you know it was my daughter?"

"A note I found with the books that once were yours, saying that you had been missing for eight years. It said your family was settling your estate. The letter was written by Joyce West."

"Yes, Joyce would donate them to the prison or some such organization. She is a good girl, always trying to help where she can."

Alan noticed Azcob's eyes were a little more watery than when he came in. A knock at the door broke the quiet tension that had built in the room.

"Come in, Azonia!"

The door opened, and she swept in beautifully with a tray containing two glasses and a pitcher of juice on it.

"Thank you, Azonia. Let me properly introduce the two of you. Azonia, this is Alan Eliot. He is from our homeland. He used Azterl's book to come here as I did before you were born. Alan, or Azearth, this is my amazing daughter, Azonia."

Both Alan and Azonia nodded to each other shyly.

Azcob continued, "My wife, the empress Azonian is out shopping at this time. I guess some things never change from world to world. Luckily, there are no credit cards here." Azcob laughed quietly.

"Let us talk now, daughter."

"Okay, Father, I will be close by if you need anything, just holler."

Alan silently wished she would stay. He found her to be astoundingly gorgeous.

Once again, the men were alone, and Azcob spoke, "Why don't you tell me all that has happened on your trips to Azor."

Alan explained what happened when he was tricked by Kasan into helping him escape and how he killed the two soldiers.

"Well, your intentions were good, so I will speak to the elders and clear you."

"Thank you, Azcob, I am truly sorry for that mistake."

Alan went on telling Azcob about meeting Azmora and Lucky and being held prisoner in Krem's castle, as well as Krhea aiding in his escape. He talked about fighting in Azden for money and his run-in with the soldiers and Azop, telling how Lucky was instrumental in his getting away. He skipped over the details about the azkibitz hideout on the mountain. Instead, he gave Azterl's entry as the reason he was looking for the book *The Pilgrim's Progress*. He said it was this search that brought him to Azing and Azterl's castle, where he discovered the book was missing. He told Azcob how he then met Aztrion and how they were captured in Azon as they traveled.

"You seem to have run a pretty impressive bluff about having magical powers. You probably have Krem and his people as worried as you have Azop and Aztrion. Azop actually came to me with his concerns about you being a wizard when his spell wouldn't work against you. They fear you may be on Krem's side. Even Aztrion said you escaped from a wagon in which you were bound and gagged.

"You mean Aztrion was able to escape while I was gone?"

"Yes, she has escaped and been recaptured twice since then. She is quite a resourceful lady."

"Did she mention what happened to my friend the azkibitz that night?"

"As a matter of fact, she did mention that the creature was able to get away."

"That is good news. I have grown very fond of that azkibitz. He has saved my life on a number of occasions."

"So, Emperor, how is it that you are able to stay here and not be drawn back automatically by the book?"

"That will take some explaining, but let me start at the beginning. It was twenty years ago that Azterl's book showed up in my private library. This would equate to ten earth years as you must know by now. My first few trips here, I wandered around and just checked things out. I didn't dare approach a town at first. Finally, on my fourth trip, I entered this town of Azkrem. It just so happened that there was a major dispute going on between a large group of townspeople. I offered a solution, and the people listened. Maybe it was because I seemed so different, and they assumed Azterl sent me to replace their recently deceased emperor. Before I knew it, I had been crowned the new emperor. I took the name Azcob because I used to smoke a corncob pipe back then. The major problem was that I had responsibilities on earth with family and business. These responsibilities kept me from coming to Azor as often as I wished. I made twenty-one trips in two years' time. I met the now empress Azonian on my tenth trip, and she found out she was pregnant with my child on my fifteenth trip. Azonia was born about a year after I first found the book, or two years in Azor time.

I had two grown children on earth, Joyce and Dickie, whose mother had passed away while they were still children. So for the most part, I was free other than business commitments. Problems popped up too often here in Azor, while and because I was gone so much. I tried to compensate by starting the hall of elders to address issues in my absence. This didn't work as well as I hoped because the people didn't accept their rulings like they did mine. The best reason I have ever been able to come up with for not getting pulled back was, maybe the book was destroyed somehow while I was here. Now that you are here, I assume it was the desire of the people to have me here that kept me. So it had been sixteen years of this new life for me.

Essentially, the people of Azor are the heartbeat of its existence, and that is a powerful force."

"Are you sorry you've been kept here?"

"No, even though I miss earth and my kids. I have a family here that needs me also."

Alan could see that Azcob did indeed miss earth, and he felt sad for the emperor. Just then, he remembered the photo of the sunset that he had brought with him. He pulled it out of his pocket and handed it to Azcob. The emperor stared at it for some time with a distant look in his eyes, as if he was recalling some distant memory. A tear rolled down Azcob's cheek. He wiped it away and put the picture down on his desk.

"Thank you, I will cherish this picture."

Alan felt a little embarrassed seeing Azcob in his moment of weakness.

"Azcob, do you possibly have any of Azterl's books from his castle library?"

"No, I wasn't even aware he had a library."

"I fear that Krem has the book I am searching for since you don't have it. I don't look forward to returning to his castle, but I must find the book."

"I don't envy you and your quest, but why didn't Azterl ever mention this book in the entries I read?"

"They are vague and obviously change with the needs of the moment."

"Yes, his entries were very vague, but seemed so obvious when you finally realize what he meant."

"Ya, sometimes I would think I made the right choice, only to find out I was totally wrong."

The emperor nodded with a look of understanding. "Would you stay for dinner? I am sure the empress would be very upset with me if she didn't meet you and get to feed you."

"I would be honored to meet the empress and stay for dinner. I don't look forward to going to Kreal anyways."

"Come on, I will show you where you can wash up, and while you do that, I will have Azonia set another place."

At dinner, Alan met the empress and was struck by her beauty and kindness. Azire had returned for dinner, and even though he didn't mention it, Alan was sure of the outcome of the fight that took place. Most of all, Alan was mesmerized by Azonia. He hung on every word she spoke and had to catch his breath when she spoke directly to him. He felt like a teenage boy, but knew he loved her from the moment he first saw her. When dinner was completed, Alan's heart felt like it had been shattered into a million pieces, each with a sharp edge stabbing him in his chest. The cause of his pain was Azire and Azonia leaving together to take a stroll through the moonlit village.

He didn't know how he could be so dumb. Azire wasn't at dinner as just a high-ranking officer, but as a suitor to Azonia.

"Can I show you to a guest room, Azearth?"

"Yes, I wouldn't get far tonight anyways, and I will return to earth in the morning, so I will start fresh when I come back to Azor."

Alan lay in bed but couldn't sleep. All he could think about was Azonia. Two hours later, he heard Azonia come in and say good night to Azire. He heard her walk past his closed door and down the hall to her room. He lay awake the rest of the night and was ready to leave when the first rays of morning light shone through the window, and he was drawn into the black nothingness.

CHAPTER FOURTEEN

As Alan fell through the black nothingness, he thought about this being his last time he would have to deal with it. His heart was no longer in it.

He wasn't thinking about the people of Azor; instead, he let his selfishness take control of his emotions. He thought, *If I can't have Azonia, I won't bother helping Azor.*

Once he felt the firmness of his bunk beneath him, he lay quietly for a few minutes, not even thinking. When the spinning ceased, he was struck by how much he sounded like Krem. *This whole thing started because Krem lost Rhea and dealt with it by wanting to destroy Azor. I need to face the fact that I am not from Azor, and these people have long-standing families and relationships, including Azonia. I went to Azor with no promises made to me, only a request for help. I will honor that request and get Azonia out of my head.*

He got out of bed, took his sneakers and sweatpants off, and decided to get some sleep till breakfast.

When breakfast was brought around, he went back to sleep, only to be awakened an hour later for his shower. After his shower, Alan slept the day away, waking to eat his meals and going back to sleep. He seemed to be emotionally and physically drained.

At six thirty, he finally got out of his bunk and washed up, brushed his teeth, and got dressed for his journey. He had about forty-five minutes to go before sunset. He gave some thought to how he would get into Krem's castle undetected and successfully search for the book.

"I assume that Krhea would help me find the book if she felt it wasn't a threat to her family by doing so. If I run into Krem, he won't be as easily bluffed as Kasan was. But then again, he did make the cell I escaped from to hold Azterl, so he will be a little leery of my supposed powers. I should probably prepare for a physical confrontation as well." He spent the next twenty minutes doing stretches and was immediately aware he hadn't stretched in a while. He made a mental commitment to stretch more consistently as it could be the difference between winning or losing a fight, or even getting injured.

Azonia popped into his thoughts, and he consciously pushed the thought from his head, but the stabbing pain remained in his chest.

"All right, Azterl, let's see what advice you have for me today." He settled down and covered his legs with his blanket to disguise the fact that he was wearing sneakers in bed. Then he reached out and picked up Azterl's book, opening it to the seventh entry.

Entry 7

Let me begin by saying, I wish I could one day lay eyes on Azor when it was completely free of threats once again.

I suppose that by now, you have become a lot more comfortable in Azor, and you are more equipped to deal with this quest. Have you come up with a solution for the problem you face yet? If not, don't be discouraged. It's only your seventh trip upcoming.

I imagine that the workings of this book must seem very confusing to you, especially, seeing as I am dead and yet still giving you relevant yet vague messages. It isn't really me talking to you. What you read isn't necessarily what I wrote. Actually, what I wrote is changed by the magic of the book to meet the reader's needs. It is hard to explain, but the simplest of explanations is that a part of me exists in the book. The book will cease to function magically when there is no longer a threat to Azor.

Sometimes, a person can deceive in the midst of trying to do good. Deceit is not always bad. Usually using your head, instead of muscle, can solve a problem with less casualties. Good luck, the people of Azor are counting on you.

Alan was sure Azterl had put his helpful advice at the end of the entry to make it easier for him. So he reread the last paragraph registering it to memory. Hopefully, this would give him some advantage.

He laid the book down and invoked Azterl's spell. Nothing happened. He didn't really expect the spell to work without the book in his possession, but he had to try. He picked the book up and invoked the spell again. This time the world fell out from under him. He kept his eyes tightly shut during his fall through the nothingness, but it didn't help much. When he felt a solid surface beneath him again, he was still nauseous, and his head was spinning. When he was finally able to open his eyes safely, Azire was sitting in a chair across from the bed he was lying in.

"Well, I thought the emperor was losing touch with reality when he asked me to stay here this morning and wait for you to show up. How did you do that? Where were you? Are you a magician as well as a fighter?"

"It is a long story, Azire. Where is Azcob and why did he have you wait for me?"

"He is up at the castle with Azop, the empress, and Azonia. There has been some trouble in the day you have been away. Aztrion has been captured right out of the castle. This caused great concern as Azkrem has been relatively safe ground up till now. Azcob said he was circling the wagons and to bring you when you show up. What is circling the wagons?"

"It just means to prepare for an attack."

"Why didn't he just say that then?"

"It's a nostalgia thing. Never mind. How far is the castle?"

"It's just outside the northern edge of town. It should take about ten minutes on the azdwarks I have out front."

"Does Azcob really think other attempts at capture are imminent?"

"He fears this will boost the confidence of Krem's men to attempt further kidnappings."

They climbed into the saddles of the waiting azdwarks and made good time to the castle as the streets were completely deserted. It was obvious an alarm had been sounded; all the shops and cottages were closed up tight. It took less than ten minutes for them to arrive at the castle. There were soldiers standing guard, who took control of the azdwarks as soon as Azire and he climbed off. Alan followed Azire at a relaxed run across the drawbridge and in through the courtyard. They jogged up a long stairwell and down a hall that was large enough to drive an eighteen-wheeler through. Alan was beginning to fall behind when Azire looked over his shoulder and slowed down for him to keep up. They came to a stairwell at the end of the hall. Azire went to go up the stairs but fell over something and landed on the stairs, banging his knee. He caught himself with his hands before smashing his face on the stone steps.

"Damn, azvars are always getting in the way. Go on now, you slimy ghost. Get out of the way!"

Alan felt something brush against his leg as he heard the familiar sucking sounds of the azvar going back down the hall from the way they had come.

"Do we have to go so fast, Azire? Is there an emergency?"

"No, but I don't like leaving Azonia unprotected for long."

This answer made Alan grimace and brought back all the pain he had felt, but Azire did proceed a little slower. At the top of these stairs was another long hallway, which they started down. Alan could see a group of six soldiers standing guard in front of a door. As they approached, the guards fell back away from the door, allowing Azire and Alan to go in. The room was huge. There were couches and chairs strewn throughout the room but all facing the center. Azcob and the empress were sitting on a couch together, and there was a man in an orange robe sitting in a chair beside their couch. He seemed distressed. Azonia was standing by a window when they came in but went to Azire's side when they entered the room. Alan ignored them, or tried to. He went to Azcob who stood as Alan approached.

"It's good to see you made it back so soon. I had Azire go wait for you to return so you wouldn't wonder where everyone went when you came back."

"Thanks for that, Emperor. What has happened? Azire told me Aztrion was taken."

"First, let me introduce you to Azop. This is Azterl's son and Aztrion's brother."

"We met in Azden briefly."

Alan reached out and shook Azop's outstretched hand.

Azop was looking at him curiously, then said, "Why do you wear the color of Krem?"

"It is hard to explain, but it is the only color I happen to have. I am not on Krem's side!"

"You are a magician, and you have been seen with Kasan. How do you explain this?"

"I will not have you question a guest of mine. I will explain everything later, Azop. But for now, this man is loyal to your father, and you will show him respect."

"I am sorry, Emperor. I am just upset about Aztrion. Can you forgive my rudeness, Azearth?"

"Yes, Azop, and I am sorry about your sister."

Azop mumbled his thanks as he turned away from Alan in heavy thought.

"Azcob, I thought you said Aztrion had been captured numerous times and always manages to get away. Why are you so worried this time?"

"Yes, it is true. But this is the first time an attempt to capture someone in Azkrem has been successful. It's like they entered our camp and walked away with one of our generals. I fear this will bolster Krem's loyalists to be even more daring."

"Where was Aztrion captured at?"

"She was here with Azop when they got her. That is why Azop is so touchy. He wasn't even aware anything was amiss until she was already gone."

"Then how do you know it was Krem or his people? Maybe she went somewhere on her own."

"We found azreyvick droppings on one of the towers."

Alan turned to Azop, saying, "Azop, do you have any idea who may have taken books from your father's library?"

"No, I didn't. I can't read his books. Why do you ask?"

"I must find a book that is missing from that library collection. I guess I will have to go to Kreal after all. At least, I can try and help Aztrion escape while I am there."

"I will go with you and help rescue my sister."

"No, I think Azcob will need you here, and it won't help if you are captured as well. I have a sure way out if I am unlucky enough to be caught. There is something you can do to help though, Azop."

"What is it? I will do whatever I can."

"I need you to put a spell on me that will make me immune to other wizard's spells."

"Why? You are a wizard! I tried to put a spell on you and couldn't."

"I was under the effect of Krhea's spell at the time."

"What do you mean, Krhea? You are awful familiar with Krem's family. Whose side are you really on?"

"Azop, I told you once—"

"But, Azcob—"

"No buts, Azop. I will not tell you again. This man is here to help, and I trust him. Put the spell on him and then be quiet please!"

"As you wish, Emperor. *Azcopop azordy!*"

"Now, Azearth, let me see you in private for a few minutes," said Azcob.

Alan followed Azcob to the opposite side of the room by the window where Azonia had been standing when they came in.

"I know you must go to Kreal, but I would like you to take Azire with you."

"No, Azcob, I am better off on my own. You know if I get caught, Azterl's book spell will help me escape as it did before."

"Well then, accept one of my azdwarks to carry you and an azrenit to send word back to me. Also, I have an aztadzhick in my employ that I will let you take to spy ahead for you."

"Thank you, I will take the azdwark, but what are the other two?"

"An azrenit is a courier bird of sorts, like a cross between an earth pigeon and parrot. This one's name is Azcal, and all you have to do is call his name, and he will come to you. I will send him following behind you. The aztadzhick is a puke-green ferret that—"

"Oh no, not one of those. I will do without the aztadzhick."

"I guess you have met one, huh?"

"Yes, I don't wish to put up with one on this trip. I would strangle it."

"I have felt the same way myself on occasion. You will have to be extremely careful traveling through Azmig and Azbec. I am sure that the second village you come to, which will be Azbec, is held by Krem. With the news of the capture here, the people may turn to Krem also out of fear."

"I will be careful and skirt around the villages if possible. How long will it take on an azdwark to reach Kreal?"

"You should reach Azmig about an hour before sundown, then Azbec somewhere in the night, maybe three or four hours before sunrise. You will have to leave shortly thereafter, so if you tie the azdwark where it can graze, it will stay until you return. When you do return, it will be seven or so hours to get to Kreal."

"I just thought of something. All the water is poisoned, so how will I supply for the azdwark's thirst?"

"They get their water from the things they eat. They are amazingly durable animals. Come now, let's get some food and drink into you."

They all went into the next room where a table was piled high with food. As they ate, Alan tried to keep his eyes from meeting Azonia's. The couple of times they did meet eyes, Alan felt the stabbing pain in his chest for what he would never have.

After they finished eating, the empress gave him a bag of fruit to carry on his trip. Then when Azcob, Azire, and Alan were outside with the azdwark, Azire showed him a pouch in the saddle to carry his bag of fruit in.

"The emperor tells me you declined an offer of me going with you, but I must ask you again myself."

"Thanks, Azire, but I must do this on my own, and you are needed here."

Azcob and Azire wished him good luck and safe passage, as he mounted and rode out over the drawbridge heading north. The path went straight into a gold forest as soon as he was away from the castle. He found that riding the azdwark was a little uncomfortable. The saddle was made for someone a foot shorter than him. He had to keep his knees bent in order to keep them in the stirrups, as you couldn't ride safely unless you kept your feet secure in them. His chest also rubbed the saddle wrong as his torso was longer than the saddle was designed for. He resolved to toughen up and ride as long and hard as he could stand. After two hours of the azdwark running at top speed, Alan was becoming aware that these things never got tired. It was as if they loved to run and the faster and longer, the better.

Three hours after leaving Azkrem, the forest ended, and the path continued on across a long meadow. Alan could see hills way off in the distance ahead. He decided to stop and give the azdwark a rest and a chance to graze. He really needed a rest himself more than anything. He reined in the animal and veered off the path onto the field of purple grass. He hadn't realized how much he had stiffened up until he climbed down from the azdwark. He lay down on the grass and stretched his legs and back. The azdwark didn't graze; he sort of just paced around like he was anxious to get running again.

Alan lay there in the grass with his eyes closed, thinking about all that had happened since finding Azterl's book. Then his thoughts turned to Azonia. *Why do I keep thinking about her? Maybe because she is the most beautiful woman I've ever seen, and it bothers the hell out of me that she doesn't even acknowledge I exist. She and Azire have probably been together since they were kids. They look close to the same age. Azire is probably a couple years older. Oh well, this isn't doing me any good. I need to focus on the mission and quit fantasizing about a relationship that isn't going to happen.*

"Come on, beast, you want to run? Let's go."

He crawled back in the saddle, and without the slightest coaxing, the azdwark started running down the path. He was almost knocked right out of the saddle by the azdwark's excitement to be running again. Alan wondered if he fell off, would the azdwark just keep running until he got hungry or ran out of path? The thought of walking to Kreal made him tighten his grip a little more.

He reached the hills after about an hour. He rode through the hill country for about two hours, and then the path led into a forest again. He decided to stop before entering the forest. He had been riding about six hours now and figured it to be around three o'clock. He reined in the azdwark and again brought him off the path into the grass. When he climbed down, he was even stiffer than before. He dug out his bag of fruit and lay in the grass eating. The azdwark grazed nearby this time. Alan recognized one of the fruits in his bag as the same kind that he saw on his first trip near the pool of water. He peeled it and threw the center fruit to the azdwark as he had seen the soldiers do. The azdwark gulped it down and looked toward Alan for more.

"There's only one, pal, sorry."

It didn't seem to understand and kept staring at him, waiting for more. Finally, it gave up and resumed grazing. Alan ate the peel, which was chewy but sweet and immediately took away his thirst. He rested for about twenty minutes, then decided he better get moving. Azcob said he should reach Azmig about an hour before sunset. He figured that would change to a half hour since he took two breaks. This was fine since he wanted to wait for dark to go through, or preferably around the village anyway.

He put the bag of fruit away in the saddle pouch and reluctantly climbed back in the saddle and urged the beast into the forest. About an hour or so later, the forest ended at the bank of a river, running right across the path. He almost flew head first into the water when he jerked the azdwark to a sliding halt.

Why the heck would they put a river across the path? It's probably one of Krem's tricks to deter trade between Azkrem, Azmig, and Azbec. Divide-and-conquer tactics, thought Alan.

The river was about fifty yards across and appeared deep. He wondered whether he should just go downstream in order to find a crossing point. The current didn't seem strong, but he was unsure as to whether the poison water would affect a swimmer, be it an azdwark or person.

"Can you swim, boy?" he asked the azdwark.

The azdwark just stood there waiting for the rider to make up his mind. Well, the animal seem to know the water is poison, at least Lucky knew. So he nudged the beast forward to see what happened. The azdwark entered the water with no hesitation, holding its head as high as it could to keep his muzzle out of the water. Alan was surprised how quickly the azdwark's six legs churning at once could get them across the river. They only drifted downstream about fifteen yards and exited the water on the opposite bank. The azdwark shook itself like a dog as soon as it hit the shore, knocking Alan right out of the saddle. He was taken by surprise and almost landed under the beast's feet. He rolled away quickly to avoid being stomped on. He got up and checked to see if the saddle was still secure once the azdwark finished stomping and shaking. The saddle was fine, but the fruit bag and fruit were soaked through. He threw it away, not knowing if it was ruined, and he wasn't willing to take a chance. He remembered clearly how Lucky had reacted to only a touching of his muzzle to the water.

Satisfied that the saddle was secure and the animal was finished shaking itself, he remounted and urged it back onto the path and into the forest again. He rode through the forest without further event for a couple of hours. It was close to sunset, and Alan began wondering if he was going to make it to Azmig before dark. Maybe he should try to find a spot for the azdwark to remain while he was gone. A few minutes later, the forest ended, and there appeared to be houses just ahead. He stopped just at the edge of the trees and surveyed the area. There were definitely houses and now that he could see more clearly on his left and right, he was convinced this was Azmig.

This village wasn't set up like Azkrem. It stretched out on both sides as far as he could see. The path ahead went between two buildings, then across a main road and between two more buildings, back into the forest. Alan figured he could shoot right across in seconds without gaining much attention and then find a place to leave the azdwark. He nudged the azdwark into a run and shot between the houses into the street. All of a sudden, Alan saw a wagon on his left that had been blocked by the house. The man pushing the wagon saw the azdwark and rider at the same time they saw him, but it was too late to stop. The azdwark ran right into the side of the wagon. The azdwark's front legs folded up beneath itself on impact, sending Alan through the air and landing face first in a heap in the middle of the intersection. Before he could even think, darkness enveloped him.

CHAPTER FIFTEEN

As Alan drifted back into consciousness, he found himself lying flat on his back, looking up into a crowd of faces. One of the men was yelling about his wagon being ruined. In a fog, he realized the man yelling was in the midst of raising some type of crude farm tool, in an attempt to strike him. Alan tried to move, but his pain-ridden body didn't respond. The tool hit him in the upper arm with such force, it cut through the flesh and muscle, right to the bone. The pain in his arm hadn't even registered yet from the deep wound when he was struck by another person with a similar tool. This one cut his stomach wide open, fueling the mob to hack him with their tools as well. All Alan could hear were his own screams of agony.

He sat up screaming and looked into the surprised faces of the crowd standing around him. They had no farm tools and made no attempts to hurt him; they just stood there, staring. It slowly dawned on him that he must have had a dream, or better yet, a nightmare while he was knocked out. He climbed to his feet and looked around for his azdwark. It was standing on the outskirts of the crowd of people. He started to head for the animal when a man stepped in his path and confronted him.

"Where do you think you're going, stranger? You must pay me for my wagon!"

"What do you mean? It was as much your fault as mine."

Alan was thinking how much easier this would be on earth. They would just exchange names and insurance companies, and be on their way. The man was ranting and raving. Even the witnesses in the crowd were arguing over what they saw and who was to blame. Alan was beginning to worry as it was turning into a mini riot in the street. He figured if he could reach the azdwark in the confusion, he may be able to make a run for it. Just as he was ready to put his plan into action, a half dozen soldiers rode up on azdwarks. The crowd slowly dispersed, leaving Alan and the wagon owner standing there, facing the soldiers.

"I won't even ask whose fault this is, as it is obvious you can't resolve this yourselves, so we will escort you both to the elders."

Alan didn't care for this delay, but the sooner it was resolved, the quicker he could be back on track. He grabbed the reins of his azdwark and led it down the street escorted by the soldiers and wagon owner. He didn't look forward to being in front of the elders again, even though these would be different ones. He was sure they wouldn't be quite as severe over an accident.

They arrived at the Hall of Elders and were immediately given an audience rather than having to wait as Alan did in Azkrem. There were also seven elders in attendance here. The oldest-looking one sat in the center of the others, and he spoke first.

"State your names and the nature of your disagreement, gentlemen."

The wagon owner said, "You know my name, Eldest Azcaliop. Everyone here knows you are my uncle, with the exception of this stranger."

"Yes, Azeclat, what you say is true, but we still must follow procedures, especially with a stranger present."

The elder turned his attention to Alan. "What is your name, stranger?"

"My name is Azearth."

"Very well, Azearth, what is the nature of your dispute? And one at a time, if you don't mind."

Azeclat started speaking before Alan had a chance, so he kept quiet, not to upset the elders. He was going to have an uphill battle with the eldest being Azeclat's uncle.

"Well, to begin with, I was approaching the center of town with my loaded push wagon, and this stranger who calls himself Azearth came out of the crossroads at a dead run. His azdwark ran right into the side of my wagon, smashing it. I worked for two months for those crops, and my wagon will have to be completely replaced."

"Okay, Azeclat, we will get into cost after we have made our decision on blame. You may give your side of the story, Azearth."

"Thank you. I was coming from Azkrem on my way to Kreal on urgent business. As I entered the crossroad at a slow gallop, this man pushed his wagon into my path, causing my azdwark to crash and me to be thrown into the street. I wish to point out I was in a position to see if anything was coming. Whereas, Azeclat was behind his wagon, pushing it into the intersection, unable to see other traffic. Furthermore, there is no right of way posted, so right or wrong must be based solely on our carelessness. I propose to you that I acted responsibly, and Azeclat acted with carelessness."

"That was a very impressive defense, Azearth. You do not mention or ask for any damages?"

"I do not have any damages as my azdwark seems fine, and you said damages would be discussed after a decision was made determining fault."

"Yes, I did, didn't I? We will have to confer among ourselves. You will be placed in cells until our decision."

Both Azeclat and Alan protested that lockup wouldn't be necessary, but the elders insisted. They were led to different cells to await their fate.

Alan started pacing in the cell, one two three four turn, one two three four turn, from the wall to the door, again and again. He thought, *Damn, here I am in jail again. Hopefully, they don't side against me. I can't pay damages without money. I wonder if they would let me earn some money by fighting to pay the damages.* Alan walked to the door and yelled out to Azeclat, "Azeclat, can you hear me?"

"Yes, I can hear you, Azearth. I am only two cells down."

"If the elders decide against me, how much is your wagon and produce worth?"

"Well, let's see. The wagon was old so that would be considered. I guess the wagon was worth about one hundred pieces when it was new, so maybe sixty pieces. The produce could have been sold for one hundred and twenty pieces in the village market. They will consider spoilage and overstock, so about ninety pieces. It would be around one hundred and fifty pieces in total. Can you pay that, Azearth?"

"No, I don't have any pieces. But I was wondering if the elders may let me win some money by fighting in one of the inns?"

"How do you plan on winning pieces by fighting?"

"In Azden, I fought at an inn where the innkeeper took bets, and when I won, he gave me fifteen pieces."

"You may have gambled in Azden. They are a motley bunch that live there. If you make the mistake of mentioning it here in Azmig, I will not even guess how the elders will punish you."

"Thanks for the advice. I will be sure not to mention it."

"Here comes the guard. By the way, they don't allow us to talk down here," he said in a hushed voice.

It wasn't a guard that showed up, but an elder. He released Azeclat from his cell, saying something to him, which Alan couldn't make out. He then came to Alan's cell.

"You have been found guilty of reckless riding inside the village limits. You have also been found guilty of causing the damage to Azeclat's wagon and produce. The cost of which is one hundred and twenty pieces. Can you pay?"

"No, I have no pieces. Can I appeal this decision? I feel that Azeclat's uncle had a lot to do with this unfair decision."

"You are right, but not exactly in the way you suggest. The vote was three to three. The three of us that are secretly loyal to Krem, voted in your favor. The deciding vote was Eldest Azcaliop's. He is loyal to Azterl and thus voted against you. We are sure he knows, as we do, that you are a spy for Krem. We all assume you are in a hurry to deliver whatever news you have acquired in Azkrem. The other elders no doubt wish to hold you here as long as they can, to prevent your message getting through."

Alan was more than a little surprised by all this, but tried not to let it show. While the elder was speaking, Alan reflected back to Azterl's words, "Sometimes a person can deceive to do good. Deceit is not always bad." So Alan decided to play along and see how this worked out.

"How did you know I was a spy? Am I that obvious?"

"In some ways, yes. You wear Krem's colors as if you were in his castle, instead of Azmig. You also openly mentioned coming from

Azkrem and going to Kreal on urgent business, which only leads people to suspect."

"What happens now? I don't have the pieces to pay. Could I trade my azdwark?"

"No, it has the saddle and bridal of Azcob, so Eldest Azcaliop suspects it is stolen and will never let you bargain with it. I suspected you wouldn't be able to pay, so I am going to assist you in your escape if you agree to tell Krem of my loyalty and help."

"I will do that, and I am sure he will be very grateful as the information I carry is of great importance."

"Okay, the guard who is on tonight is secretly loyal to Krem also. It is now one hour after sunset, so when I bring the news back to the elders that you can't pay, they will go home for the night. The guard will then make a round and walk close to your cell. He will allow you to grab him, pulling him into the bars, knocking him unconscious. Do it for real, for the sake of everyone to see. When he falls, reach out and take the keys to let yourself out. Lock him in the cell. Do not open any other cells. Go up the stairs to the hall and let yourself out the back door, which I will leave unlocked. On second thought, just kick it open since I am the key holder and will be suspected if the door were left open. When you get out the door, turn to your right, and the fourth building you come to will be the stable. You will be on your own there, but you should be able to get your azdwark. When you exit the stable, continue to the right until you get to the crossroad where the accident took place. Turn left onto the path, which will take you to Kreal, or I should say, Azbec and then Kreal. We hold Azbec, so you will have no trouble there wearing Krem's color. I must go let the elders know we are done for the night. Good luck and don't forget to tell Krem how I helped."

"Thank you, I will tell him."

The old man turned and left with a look of satisfaction and impending importance on his face. Alan figured the elder sought to become Eldest by helping Krem when he eventually took over. Wouldn't he be surprised if he knew the truth. Alan laughed out loud at this thought and one of the other prisoners yelled for him to shut up.

Alan sat in his bunk waiting for the guard to make his round. About ten minutes passed when he heard the guard coming. Alan went to the side of the cell door and waited. The guard walked obviously close to the cell door, and Alan grabbed him by his uniform, pulling him and his head straight into the bars.

"The guard yelled, "Hey, what are you doing? Let go of me!"

Alan grabbed him by the back of the head and pulled the man's head into the bars with a loud crack. This time the guard's unconscious body sunk to the floor. Alan took the keys off the guard's belt and let himself out of the cell. He then dragged the guard into the cell and locked him in. When he stepped out into view, the other prisoners all started cheering and yelling for him to let them out also. Alan remembered what the elder had said and hurried past them and up the stairs. When he got to the top of the stairs, he stopped, turned around, and ran back down. As he reached the first occupied cell, he threw the keys into the man standing there and said, "I am in a hurry. Let the others out also." Then he ran back up the stairs and down the hall to the back door. It took two quick kicks for the door to fly open. It was so quiet outside that he paused for a second before taking off at a run to the right as instructed. The fourth building was no doubt the stable. He could smell as well as hear the azdwarks. He had to go right out on the main street to access the building. There were two huge doors with a smaller door built into one of them. Alan tried the door, and it opened. He ducked inside and let his eyes adjust to the low light before going any farther. There were stalls on both sides of the building, and each one housed an azdwark. He walked down through the stalls, but all of them looked alike. Then he noticed that the saddles hung on the stalls, but the bridals were still on the animals. The saddles were all different in color and design. He recognized Azcob's black saddle, so he opened the stall door and led the azdwark out by the reins. Just as he was ready to grab the saddle off the wall mount, the double doors opened, and a man stood there leading an azdwark. The light of the moon flooded the stable, and the man spotted Alan.

"Hey! What are you doing there?"

Alan didn't stop to respond. He jumped up onto the azdwark's back with a little difficulty and headed it toward the man and door. The man jumped out of the way, just as Alan's azdwark bounced off the other azdwark and out the door. Alan pulled hard on the reins to the right, almost slipping from the animal's back as it turned sharply. He grabbed a handful of the thick shaggy fur with one hand and held the reins with the other. He lay on his stomach and hugged the beast back with his legs and arms. When he reached the crossroads, he turned left onto the path leading into the forest. As he looked back, he could see the stable man yelling and pointing him out to a group of soldiers. The soldiers were busy with a half dozen men Alan assumed were the other escapees.

The azdwark broke into a full run without any urging from Alan. He let the animal run as fast as it wished and concentrated on holding on tightly. His face was pressed into the neck of the azdwark, and the smell was more than he could take. He was also getting whipped in the head by the animal's long hair catching the wind. Regardless of this, he held on tight in this position for at least an hour. Finally, he decided to stop, as his legs and arms were on fire and cramped from holding on so tightly. He was afraid that if his muscle gave out and he fell off at this speed, he would die or be seriously injured. There were no fields or meadows in sight, or at least not in the ten yards he could clearly make out. There had been nothing except forest on both sides since they turned onto the path in Azmig.

He reined the animal to a halt and climbed down. He almost fell flat on his face as his legs weren't working quite right. He lifted his legs and squatted a few times until the feeling flowed back into them along with the blood. Then he led the azdwark into the trees a little bit in case they were being followed. As he rested, he realized how hungry and thirsty he was. He hadn't even noticed prior because of the adrenaline flowing through him. There was nothing he could do about it now, and the azdwark was probably fed at the stable.

He tried to calculate the time he lost while in Azmig, which equated to four hours, give or take. Azcob predicted he would arrive in Azbec about three hours before sunup, so now he should be an hour out of Azbec at sunrise when he gets pulled out of Azor. He would have to find a place for the azdwark to graze while he was gone.

"Well, come on, buddy. It doesn't appear we were followed."

Alan led the azdwark back to the path, mounted it, and they were off at a full run again. The forest continued about a half hour further, and then Alan could see a meadow ahead. As soon as they entered the meadow, the azdwark suddenly changed its style of running. It didn't slow down at all, but its gallop became so out of sync it was difficult for Alan to hold on. The azdwarks usually moved all three legs on one side together and then the other three together when walking, giving him a side-to-side gait. Each gear or speed that the azdwark reached would require a different combination of legs being used. For instance, when the animal sped up, he would use the four front legs, then follow with the two back legs, more like pulling himself along. When his speed picked up further, he would switch to using two front legs first then pushing himself forward with four hind legs. This latter mode created great torque and powerful speed. Since entering the meadow, the azdwark wasn't using any of the familiar modes of running. He was landing on only one of the six legs at a time and in no given pattern that Alan could discern. This scared him, as it didn't seem at all safe. He was also worried that the animal may have come up lame and just refused to stop. As he was looking down toward the animal's feet to see if he could detect an injury, he realized the real reason for the odd gait, and it scared him even more. The meadow Alan had thought they entered wasn't a meadow after all; it was a swamp. The azdwark was running on pieces of rock jutting up out of the water about an inch above the surface. Each column of rock was only about six inches across, just big enough for the azdwark's three-toed foot to stand on. The stone columns seemed to be randomly placed, but the azdwark had no problem traversing on them. Alan wished the animal would slow down a little, but didn't dare distract it by even blinking. He even found himself holding his breath for a long time. This went on for a half hour, and finally, Alan just shut his eyes as he couldn't watch the columns any longer. They were becoming a blur. He ridiculously thought this blurring of his vision would cause the azdwark to misstep.

After what seemed an eternity, but was only about fifteen minutes, the azdwark resumed its normal mode of running. They were in the forest again, and Alan decided to take a short break even though the azdwark didn't seem the least bit bothered by their trek through the swamp.

This azdwark never seems to get tired, Alan thought. He pulled the animal to a halt and climbed down, landing in a heap on the ground as his legs wouldn't hold his weight. He really must have been squeezing tight to the point of muscle failure, to keep from falling off. His throat was burning when he swallowed, and his thirst was multiplied by the fact that he had nothing to quench it. He decided he would have to toughen up and get as far as he could in the six or so hours before sunrise.

He picked himself up and stretched, then climbed back onto the beast. He figured they would stop at the next field or meadow so the azdwark could eat. The animal seemed more than happy to be on its way again. They rode through the forest for another hour before finally coming to a meadow. Alan steered the azdwark off the path and climbed down carefully this time and lay in the grass.

The azdwark grazed nearby as Alan watched him. He decided to try a couple of strands himself. The grass was bitter, but it contained moisture, which he needed badly. He dozed off to sleep for a couple of minutes only to be awakened by a horrible bleating sound. He recalled hearing this sound in the forest the day he fought with Azire and the other soldiers. He scrambled to his feet, searching for the cause of the sound. The azdwark was about twenty-five yards away and appeared to be under attack but frozen at the same time. Alan ran within ten yards of the animal and then froze also when he caught sight of the attacker. The creature was half the size of the azdwark and as black and hairy as the azdwark, but it had claws, which are at least a foot long. Alan could clearly see the bloody claws slashing back and forth in the moonlight as it dug into the azdwark's back. The azdwark seemed to be frozen in fear, as it just stood there bleating its death scream.

"Get out of there! Hey you, beat it!" Alan screamed, waving his arms.

He remembered Azmora telling him about the azdirktooths, just as the creature turned its head to look at him. Alan's shouts froze in his throat when he saw the huge teeth jutting from the animal's mouth. The teeth were eight inches long and came to a needlepoint, with bright-red blood dripping off them. Alan wanted to do something for the helpless azdwark, but he remembered Azterl's words of advice, "Usually using your head, instead of muscle, can solve a problem with less casualties."

Alan realized the only casualty being avoided here was his own. Suddenly, the azdwark's bleating stopped as the azdirktooth sunk his razor teeth into the animal's neck. This appeared to be a good time to make an exit, so Alan ran into the forest climbing a tree to the very top. He hoped the azdirktooth couldn't climb, or that it would be satisfied with the azdwark filling his foul stomach.

He wished he had chosen a tree where he could keep an eye on the azdirktooth, but he wasn't about to climb down to find a better vantage point. As he sat there, he thought about how he would get to Kreal upon his return, when he remembered the parrot-type bird Azcob called the azrenit and was supposed to have sent after him. He called out, "Azcal." He didn't dare call too loudly or repeatedly, in fear of attracting the azdirktooth. He waited ten minutes, and just as he was going to call out again, a beautiful, tiny, fluorescent pink bird landed on a branch beside him. At first, Alan wasn't sure how to give the bird a message, but he remembered Azcob described it like a parrot. He decided it probably just repeats what was said to it.

"Azcob, I am in trouble. I am in a meadow about three hours beyond Azmig. My azdwark has been eaten by what I believe to be an azdirktooth. I am up in a tree and safe, but it will be morning in a few hours, and I will have to leave. I would appreciate any help you could send in the time during my absence. Boy, do I have a story to tell you about Azmig. Thanks, in advance for your anticipated assistance, Azearth." Alan wasn't sure if his message was too long or not, but after just a minute, the bird began repeating his message verbatim, but in a squeaky bird voice. The bird then flew away.

Alan sat in the tree the rest of the night and was very happy to see the first sliver of light signifying dawn's arrival.

CHAPTER SIXTEEN

Alan didn't mind the fall through the black nothingness. He just wanted to get back to earth. He needed to quench his thirst, eat, and get some sleep. When he felt his bunk under him, he lay there quietly, allowing the spinning to come to a complete stop. Finally, he got up and drank two cups of water, which tasted like sweet honey to his parched throat. He made a cup of coffee and a packet of instant oatmeal to hold him over till breakfast was brought around. He sat on his bunk with his back against the wall drinking his second coffee. He hoped Azcob received his message and would be able to send help before he returned. He especially didn't want to be on foot with that azdirktooth scrounging around. It was still about fifteen hours on an azdwark to reach Kreal, with a town held by Krem along the way. That wouldn't leave much time to try to find Aztrion and release her, as well as search out the book. Aztrion's freedom must come first. She may be able to help me find the book, and having a wizardess around never hurts. I suppose I could have just taken Azop along if I needed a wizard, but I was too busy trying to impress Azonia with my solo efforts. I guess I let my ego get in the way of the bigger picture. I also don't really trust Azop. He is under control for the most part with Azcob around, but there is no telling what he is capable of if left unchecked.

He decided to stay awake this morning since it was shower day, and he just wasn't feeling tired. He had been neglecting his letter writing and his workout regimen of pushups and stretching, so he did this until breakfast was brought around. Breakfast consisted of two cold pancakes, an eight-ounce carton of milk and prunes, which he didn't like or eat. He was still hungry upon finishing the meal but would just have to wait for lunch.

He grabbed the letter that he received from his grandmother recently and reread it. The letter said that her car had an issue, which she couldn't afford to fix at this time, so it may be a while before she could come visit. Alan wished he were able to give her whatever she needed. His grandma Rose was always there for him for as long as he could remember.

He drifted off into thought about the gold trees on Azor and wondered if it would be possible to bring some back with him. I suppose I could bring my shank next trip and scrape some gold off one of the trees. I wonder if it would return to its original form, and I will get back here with a pocket full of wood shavings. He sat down and wrote a letter to her, telling her not to worry. He was doing good. He wished he could share some stories about Azor with her, but she would really be worried about him then.

Once he completed the letter, he decided to catch a few winks until they got to his cell for showers. He was awakened by the sound of lunch being passed around, and he asked the guard, "What happened to showers?"

"You slept through your shower."

"Are you kidding me! We don't get showers for two more days. Gimme a break, will you?"

"I am not a babysitter. We came by, and you were sleeping. That's that. Don't blame me."

"Yeah, thanks for nothing, dude."

Alan took his meal, and even though he felt like throwing it in the guard's face, he just sat down and ate. After eating, he went back to sleep until dinner was brought around. He got up and ate, then spent a whole hour taking a shower in his sink with the bubbler faucet. Basically, it was a bird bath with a dribble of water.

Alan then dug through his legal work to find his piece of flat steel that he had sharpened into a shank. He got dressed in his sneakers and sweatpants. He stuck the shank in his sock and drank a couple of cups of water, then lay down to read Azterl's book just as the sun was going down.

He turned to the eighth entry and read.

Entry 8

I believe I shall take this time to familiarize you with Krem. I think it will prove helpful if you know your enemy well.

Krem and I were friends for many years, almost from birth. We grew up in the same small village of Salem. There was this woman who practiced magic in her cottage just outside of town who everyone was afraid of. No one really went near her, and the children were forbidden to go even two hundred yards from her house. Most of the other kids didn't *need* to be forbidden as they were scared out of their minds. Krem and I dared each other to approach her one day and learned right away that the rumors were just overblown stories. She wasn't a devil worshipper; as a matter of fact, she was a God-fearing woman who read to us from the Bible often. She taught us that it was God who gave all of us our power. The power just has to be developed and honed carefully, as it could cause harm to others. We spent over thirty years together, practicing and strengthening our powers under the tutelage of Lady Victoria. She was hundreds of years old when we were with her, and she probably still lives in your time now.

Eventually, people became so prejudiced against what they believed to be devil worship and witches that they hunted them down and burned them. It was horrible and such a tragedy, and all that was left for us was to flee. We could have fought back with our magic, but Lady Victoria taught us well that God's gift should not be turned on his people for harm. We also knew fighting would only increase the falsehood and fear surrounding our gift. Krem and I decided to create Azor, a place where people could live without fear of judgment and be free to develop their God-given powers. It had been six hundred Azor years, and still, the people had walls of doubt that blocked their true abilities. The power of the mind was amazing—both in its ability to hinder as well as grow. Everyone had the power, but most also had a healthy dose of doubt.

Both Krem's children and my own had use of their powers, but even they had the block of doubt holding them back from realizing their true potential.

I hope this short history lesson helps you in your quest to assist the people of Azor. Good luck.

Alan sat there giving thought to Azterl's history lesson before invoking the spell. He thought, *If the power is in us or our minds, then how did Azterl hide his powers to be transferred to someone when the riddle is solved? Maybe the power is in our soul, and he hid his soul. But what if I am successful at finding the book and solving the riddle? Will the person I designate then have two souls? Will the two souls fight, and one become dominant? Or will they blend and work together? There are so many unanswered questions. I know Azterl is a good person, and I assume he knows what he was doing, so I'll have to trust him. I need to find the book first, or it doesn't matter.*

He lay down and covered his legs before invoking the spell. He felt the world drop out from under him, and as he fell through the black nothingness, his thoughts wandered to Azonia. He felt a hard surface beneath him, and in the next instant, he was falling. He opened his eyes only to find everything spinning out of control. He felt his body crash into one hard surface after another, knocking the wind out of him. He instinctively tucked his chin to his chest and covered his head with his arms to protect his skull from getting smashed. As he smashed off one surface after another, he realized what was happening. He arrived back where he had left from up in the tree that he had climbed to avoid the azdirktooth. Just then, he smashed into something and felt himself blacking out. When he came to again, he was lying on the ground in a heap. He had a disgusting coppery taste in his mouth, as a result of throwing up while unconscious.

"Damn, how could I be so stupid? I could have been killed or choked to death on my own vomit."

Every part of his body hurt. He moved each limb to assure himself he hadn't broken anything. He pressed on his rib cage, and his ribs were sore but not broken. He would feel it tomorrow, but he would live.

"Well, I see you're alive even though you smell as if you were dead."

Alan was startled into a sitting position by the unexpected voice and immediately regretted his movement. Pain shot through his body as he looked for the source of the voice. Azop was sitting in the purple grass about ten yards away.

"I suppose Azcob got my message and sent you, huh?"

Azop answered sarcastically, "I guess it's a good thing I stayed behind to help, so I could come rescue you."

Alan let Azop's sarcasm go unanswered as it wouldn't help getting into a verbal duel with him.

"I am grateful for your help and thankful Azcob sent you. I don't see any riding beasts though. Don't you think it would have been wise to bring a new one for me to travel on to Kreal?"

"I came here by magic and will use magic to get you on your way. First, I want you to answer a question or two."

"Okay, Azop, if it will help to quell your sarcasm and distrust of me, then ask away."

"First of all, Azcob says you are loyal to my father, but how do you know my father?"

"I don't actually know your father personally, but I am loyal to him and his cause. I came from your dad's homeland, where I found a message from him asking for help, and here I am to help."

"When did you get this message from my father?"

"I only received it recently, but it was sent before his disappearance."

"Why would he send a message to you?"

"It wasn't sent to me specifically. It was by chance I found it."

"Why do you wear the color of Krem?"

"I agree this is similar to Krem's color, but I have no choice in the color of my clothes. Think about it. It doesn't benefit me to be stuck with this color."

"I guess you are right. I suppose I should trust Azcob's opinion about you."

"It would be better for our cause if we were on the same side."

Alan stepped forward with his hand outstretched as a sign of friendship. Azop quickly stepped back away from him and spoke.

"*Azimo azclen.*"

The smell and bile instantly disappeared from Alan's body, and Azop stepped forward, shaking Alan's hand.

Once Alan realized Azop hadn't turned him into a toad or something worse, he said, "Thanks, the smell was getting to me also, and I was wondering how I would clean myself up."

"You're welcome. Now I should be getting you on your way to Kreal."

"You're not coming along? I assumed since you are here that you would join me."

"No. Azcob made me promise to help you on your way and then return to him. He has a lot of confidence in you succeeding on your own. I hope he is right, and I hope you bring my sister out safely. She has been captured many times and has succeeded in escaping each time. I am worried this time though because it has been days. She usually gets away by now."

"I promise I will do all I can, Azop. I wish I had the confidence in myself that Azcob has in me. You are right that I should get going as I have fifteen hours of travel to reach Kreal."

"Not the way I will send you. It will be a third of that."

"Oh no, I am not looking forward to this."

"You will be safe. I imagine you also want the spell of immunity to other wizards' magic as well, and you'll need some food. *Azcopop azordy, azish azendic.*"

A large bag appeared hanging over Alan's shoulder. He looked into it and found it filled with fruit. The smell and bile were gone, but the coppery taste remained, so he bit into one of the fruits. It quenched his thirst and rinsed the foul taste away.

Azop spoke again, "*Azhi azflo* Krem's castle *azlo azlan!*"

Alan felt himself slowly lifted into the air. "Hey, what the hell are you doing?"

"Don't worry, Azearth. You will float to Krem's castle and land on one of the towers safely."

Alan had floated to twice the height of the trees as Azop talked and was now moving north through the air.

"What if the spell screws up?"

Azop didn't answer his question. He only yelled, "Good luck," then disappeared.

Alan thought, *Damn you, Azop. You did this on purpose. He could have at least given me a warning. I shouldn't complain. I have always wanted to fly, and this is kind of neat. The ground below is going by at quite a clip, so Azop was not joking when he said I'll arrive in a third of the time.*

He felt no resistance from the air as he went through. It was as if the air around him was trapped in a bubble and moved with him. He was still standing straight up, so he attempted to change position and found he could easily move however he wished. He was now lying on his stomach in midair and put his arms forward like Superman. He laughed out loud and put his arms to the sides while making an airplane noise. He actually laughed at himself as he pictured how he must look. Next, he attempted a somersault and pulled it off perfectly. He was surprised he had such control of his movements. He had seen people in zero gravity on television, but they didn't seem to have control. They just floated. He could do anything, and his body just continued on north no matter which way he faced.

After two hours of floating along and enjoying himself, he passed over a town which had to be Azbec. He went over so fast that all he was able to make out were the cottages and some fenced-in areas. Then he was over the forest again for another hour of uneventful flying. He decided he would try stretching and going through his martial arts movements, blocks, and strikes. It was so much easier like this with no gravity or resistance. He spent the next hour and a half doing these exercises without tiring in the least bit. He figured he was only about a half hour from Kreal as the sun was straight overhead. In realizing he was so close to Kreal, he thought of something which hadn't entered his mind prior, What if he came upon an azreyvick. How do you defend yourself against something that size? He started paying more attention to his surroundings and felt his ankle area to see if his shank was still in his sock. The feel of the metal blade made him feel better, but not a lot. Then he remembered he forgot to get the gold scrapings from the trees as he had planned. He resolved to try to remember before going back on this trip.

Alan could now see Krem's castle in the distance. It grew larger every second until he was just above one of the towers. He stopped and was slowly lowering down and landed on the tower. He took a step forward as he felt his feet touch, and everything was normal, so he quickly ran across the roof to a doorway and ducked into the shadows. The stairs he encountered went down sharply as he hurried cautiously down them. Upon reaching the bottom, he peeked out into the hallway. He couldn't hear anyone, and there was no one in the hall. He wondered if Krem had azvars guarding his castle like others did. He had no way of bribing the creature if he ran into one.

I have to find where they are holding Aztrion, he thought. *I can't just go knocking on these doors or calling her name. Anyone could be in these rooms.*

At the end of the hallway was another stairwell. This one went both up or down, and he assumed up only led to another tower, so down he went. He exited onto another hallway and walked partway down the hall until he could see clearly that all the doors were closed also. He turned around, went back in the stairwell, and down to the next level. He entered yet another hallway and wandered down a ways. He noticed a door with a lockset in it, but all the other doors had no locks.

Alan thought, *This must be the room Kasan held me in during our fight sessions. Maybe Aztrion is in there.* He went right up to the door and pressed his ear to it, listening intently. All he could hear was his own heartbeat. He took a chance and lightly knocked, whispering Aztrion's name. When there was no response, he turned and headed for the stairs again. When suddenly, Krhea materialized before his eyes right in his path. They stood staring at each other just inches apart. Alan went to speak, but Krhea covered his mouth lightly with her hand to silence him. She took him by the hand, leading him to the stairway and up to the next floor where he had just been. She let go of his hand shyly and waved for him to follow her. They quietly went down the hall to the third door on the right. After she closed the door behind them, she led him to a chair beside the bed and motioned for him to sit down.

"Stay quiet. I'll be right back," whispered Krhea as she disappeared into thin air.

Alan sat there, not daring to move. A few minutes passed and then a few more passed. Krhea appeared before him, startling him.

"It is okay to talk now. I just had to check where my father and brothers were. What are you doing here? You are lucky I found you as Kalem was only two doors away from where we met in the hall. If I weren't so picky about keeping the castle clean, I wouldn't have found you. I stay in tune with the castle monitoring it for azvars. They often sneak into the castle and try to live here, but I pick up their presence and run them out. I sensed your movement, and thinking you were an azvar, I came to investigate."

"I am glad you did. I wasn't getting anywhere on my own and probably was destined to run head first into your father or brothers. To answer your question of why I am here, I came to free Azterl's daughter Aztrion and find a book I hope is here in the castle."

"What would Aztrion be doing here?"

"She was captured by your father's people a number of days ago, and I assumed she was being held here."

"If there was a prisoner here, I would know about it, and I assure you, there isn't."

"I believe you, Krhea. They must be holding her elsewhere. Do you have any idea where such a prisoner would be held?"

"No, I have no idea. A wizard would normally be held here in the cell you were in. You were the last prisoner held here at the castle."

This confused Alan, but he was sure she wasn't lying to him.

"Okay then, I need to find a book. Where does your father keep his books?"

"In his study, but that's where he is now and probably will remain for days. Once he goes in there, he tends to stay for days. He is doing some kind of research."

"Well, that's just great. What do I do now? Could you get him to leave the study for a little while so I can search for this particular book?"

"I can't think of a reason he wouldn't be suspicious of, as I can handle whatever comes up. If there was an issue, he would pop out of his study, dispose of the problem, and pop right back in, catching you."

"Are both of your brothers here in the castle right now? You said Kalem was in his room. Is Kasan here also?"

"Yes, he was down in the fighting room working out when I checked. What is it you are after, Alan? I can't help you if you try to hurt my family."

"You told me before that you believe the people of Azor should be free. I am trying to accomplish just that without causing anyone harm. I must find Aztrion and free her also. I believe you when you say she is not here, but either your father or brothers know where she is."

"I will help you, but you must know that if you place any of my family in danger, I will have to go against you myself."

"Yes, I know that and appreciate your help. I have to think. Can you do me a favor while I am thinking how to proceed?"

"What do you need?"

Alan reached into his sock and took out his shank handing it to Krhea.

"Can you pop out to a tree and use this to scrape off some of the gold and bring it back to me?"

"What? You want me to go get you gold scrapings from a tree?" Krhea said, looking hurt.

"Please I need it for an experiment."

"Hold your hands out, Alan."

Krhea put the shank in his right hand and said, "*Kaust kimi.*"

Scrapings of gold materialized in Alan's left hand. He was surprised, but it felt like a *duh* moment now, as she was a wizardess.

"Here is your gold. You must think I am naive, to not realize you were just trying to send me on a wild azkibitz chase for worthless gold. Well, I am neither naive nor stupid, if you want to be left alone, so be it!"

She was gone before Alan could open his mouth to explain.

Alan thought to himself, *I guess women are the same everywhere. They get upset easily and always have to have the last word.*

He put the gold scrapings in his pocket and sat on the bed to think.

"What can I use from Azterl's entry that would help me? He gave me a history lesson about Krem and him and Lady Victoria for a reason." He sat contemplating for a half hour or so, till he was finally satisfied with a somewhat risky plan. He would need a lot of luck and Krhea's help, but it just might work. He was pacing back and forth getting restless when Krhea popped back into the room. Her eyes were puffy and red. This made Alan feel like an idiot, but thought it best not to let on that he was aware of her crying. He didn't want to embarrass her further, and he needed her trust if his plan was going to work.

"I am glad you are back, Krhea. I have come up with a plan of sorts. Would you be able to pop Kasan from where he is into your father's study?"

"Yes, but why?"

"Is it difficult for you to do?"

"No, it is a very short distance."

"Could you pop yourself and Kalem there as well?"

"Yes, I can do all you ask, but you have not answered why you want me to do this."

"First, answer one more question, then I will explain. Would they be able to tell it was your magic that brought them there?"

"No, not unless I told them."

"Okay, this is my plan. I would like you to bring me to a room close to your father's study, then pop Kalem, Kasan, and yourself into the study. I will enter and speak to all of you together. I just ask that you not give my secret away. I promise no harm will come to anyone on my part. Will you trust me and do as I ask?"

"Yes. You obviously wish that it appear you brought us all together. Why don't you just do it yourself?"

"I can't do it, Krhea. If I am to expect your trust, I must be honest with you as well. I don't have any powers."

"Surely you joke with me as before."

"No, Krhea, I am serious. I have only the ability to leave this world, and I can't even control that. It happens automatically. I bluffed your brother into thinking I have powers."

"You are a strange man, Alan, but I believe you are sincere. Shall we go to the room by the study now? I will pop us there."

Alan remembered Azop's protection from magic spell, so he asked if they could just walk. Krhea agreed, so they left the room, went down the three levels of stairs, and entered a hallway.

"That door is my father's study," Krhea whispered while pointing to a door on the left side of the hall. Then she led him to a door directly across from it on the right and entered.

"Are you sure about this, Alan?"

"Not really, but let's go."

"Okay, Kasan *ketala*! Kalem *ketala*! They are both in the study now with my father. Here I go. Good luck, Alan." She reached out, squeezed his hand, and was gone.

Alan opened the door, walked across the hall, taking a deep breath, and opened the door to the study.

CHAPTER SEVENTEEN

As Alan entered the study, he was struck by two things: the size of the small room and the surprised look on everyone's faces in the crowded study. Everyone was arguing when he walked in. Now they all quietly stared at him. Krem sat at his desk, looking tired and less shocked than Kasan and Kalem. Krhea just looked nervous and uncertain. Kasan and Kalem began to put up a nervous, uncertain protest, but Krem stood, faced Alan, and quieted them both.

"Your shock-and-awe technique has achieved its goal. I wouldn't have expected less from you based on the stories I have been told concerning you," said Krem. He directed his attention to his three children, "All of you can leave now. The show of strength is over. Krhea, could you bring a cold drink for our guest and I while we talk?"

"Yes, Father, right away." She barely finished her words as she disappeared.

Both Kalem and Kasan protested, claiming Alan was dangerous. Krem spoke a couple of quiet words, and both men disappeared as quickly as their sister had seconds before.

"Have a seat, young man. It appears we have some things to discuss." He knocked a pile of stuff out of an old chair and pushed the chair toward Alan.

Alan waited until Krem turned his chair and sat facing him before taking a seat himself. He felt a little out of his league here and Krem had thrown a wrench in his plan by dismissing everyone straight away. He had hoped to use the element of surprise to keep them off balance long enough to find out about Aztrion's whereabouts.

Both men looked at each other, up and down, neither willing to speak first. Alan thought that Krem was exactly how he imagined him to be: strong, oozing authority, and even regal. Alan didn't expect the wizard to appear so obviously tired. He had the countenance of a man who got far too little sleep and had the weight of the world on his shoulders. Alan felt a little sorry for this one time pillar of society.

He decided to break the silence. "I would like to begin by asking about Aztrion's whereabouts. Do you have her here at the castle?"

Krem looked confused and shook his head. "I don't have her here or anywhere! Why would I have Azterl's daughter?"

"She was captured by your people right in the heart of Azkrem." As Alan said this, he could clearly see Krem knew nothing of this.

"If something as important as that was true, I would surely be aware. I don't make it a habit of picking on my enemy's daughter. When we finished our conversation, I will look deeper into this. For now, tell me your intentions with the dramatic entrance. What business do you wish to discuss? I am already growing weary of this encounter."

Alan decided to cut right to the chase. "I am from your old homeland, and though I don't know all about you, I have some insight into what is driving your desire to destroy Azor."

Wizard Krem appeared to grow before Alan's eyes as his anger was stoked to life by Alan's words.

"How dare you tell me you understand what drives me or my goal. You sound like Azterl. He thought he could "talk me down" as he put it. My anger and issues are far greater than you or him could ever comprehend."

Just as Alan thought Krem was going to attack him physically, there was a quiet knock on the study door. Krhea's tiny voice asked, "Can I come in, Father? I have brought the drinks you requested."

Hearing Krhea's voice seemed to deescalate Krem's anger as quickly as it had risen.

The tired wizard responded calmly, "Come in, Krhea."

Alan was thankful for the interruption and smiled at Krhea as she brought the drinks in, handing one to him and one to her father. She blushed and bowed her head as Alan smiled and thanked her.

"Do you need anything else, Father?"

Krem looked lovingly at his daughter, thanked her, and sent her on her way. Just as she was about to close the door of the study, Krem said, "Krhea, do you know anything about Azterl's daughter Aztrion being held by anyone associated with us?"

"No, Father, I haven't heard any talk about her at all."

"Tell your brothers that when I am through here, I will be summoning them, so don't go out."

"Yes, Father."

Krem turned his attention to Alan once again, "What exactly do you want from me?"

Alan thought for a moment and then tried a different tactic, "Do you think that Lady Victoria is proud of what you are doing here?" Alan expected another blow up of anger, but Krem only sat as if in deep thought.

Finally, Krem spoke, "Is she still alive? I have wondered about her often."

Alan had been planning on using her as part of his bluff. After seeing Krem's reaction to the mention of her, he decided against it. Instead, he said, "Krem, I don't know if she is still around or not. I do know she was a very important person in your life and a positive role model. That is the reason I mention her, hoping to reach that nostalgic good place in you. I can't begin to say I understand what you have suffered over the years, but I do know you and Azterl created a most amazing world together. That, I am sure Lady Victoria would be proud of you both for accomplishing."

"She taught us so much and was like a mother to us both. I wish things could be different, but I can never forgive Azterl for what he did. He was jealous, irresponsible, and vindictive. He took the life of someone greater than both of us put together."

Alan couldn't comprehend the pain in Krem's face and voice as he spoke of something so many years in the past. It was as if Rhea's accident happened yesterday.

Alan cautiously asked, "Would Rhea want Azor to be destroyed for her sake? Isn't it enough for you that Azterl is dead now? Isn't he the one you blame? It's not the innocent people of the land you created to escape tyranny and injustice, right? Aren't you doing and being what you came here to get away from?"

Alan thought he had gone too far when Krem rose from his chair coming toward him. Krem passed right by him reaching for the door handle. He said over his shoulder, "Let's go see about some food and follow up on Aztrion's whereabouts before you are on your way."

With that being said, Krem stepped through the opened door without even waiting for Alan to follow. Alan jumped up and hurried through the door and down the hall to catch up to Krem. They walked without talking, down a hall, down some stairs, and into a large dining hall. Alan had not seen this part of the castle before now. It was beautifully decorated and immaculately clean. Krhea was wiping down one of the statues lining the walls as they walked in. She looked up, and while putting her cleaning cloth away she said, "Are you ready to eat, Father?"

"Whenever you are ready, Krhea."

She shuffled out of the room quickly, just as Alan realized Kasan was sitting in a high-backed chair on the other end of the room. Krem directed Alan to a seat at the table as he sat at the head. He raised his voice and called out to Kalem, who was nowhere in sight at the moment.

Krhea entered the dining area again arms loaded with plates heaped with food. She set them on the table and removed napkins from the plates in front of her father and Alan.

"Krhea, where is your brother?"

"I don't know, Father. I am sure he heard you calling."

"Kasan, are you going to join us, or just sit there brooding?" asked Krem.

While Kasan approached the table, Krem questioned him about Aztrion.

"Father, I don't know anything about where she is or who may be holding Aztrion."

As Kasan was speaking, Kalem entered the room overhearing the last of Kasan's words.

"She hasn't returned yet?" Kalem shouted to no one in particular.

Everyone in the room spun their heads toward Kalem, shocked by his outburst.

Before anyone could even react or say anything. Kalem mumbled a quick apology and disappeared from the room.

"What was that all about? Does anyone know what's going on around here?" Krem demanded.

No one spoke. Everyone just looked at one another and shrugged.

"I am sure he'll be back soon enough, Father. Should we eat for now while we wait?"

"Why not, eating is the only thing that makes sense." Krem bowed his head and gave thanks while asking for wisdom and tolerance to deal with the mysteries surrounding him these days. He thanked Jesus, the Holy Spirit, and God, finishing with a hearty amen.

Everyone dug in at the same time that Krhea attempted to serve.

"Gentlemen, act civilized please!" She took over, offering food from each tray to each person in turn. There was no doubt who was in charge in the dining area.

They ate quietly, but there was an eerie feeling in the room the longer they waited for Kalem's return. Kasan watched Alan with suspicion written all over his face. Alan pretended not to notice.

When they finished eating, Kasan excused himself as Krem and Alan moved to the more comfortable high-backed chairs.

"So, Alan, tell me about the old homestead. Have they grown up yet, or are they still prejudiced against what they don't understand?"

"Father, can I sit and listen?" asked Krhea.

He motioned to one of the empty chairs, and Alan began telling all that he could explain about Earth. He was interrupted often with questions by both Krem and Krhea to explain something more extensively.

After about two hours, Kalem appeared were he had left from earlier. He walked toward them and collapsed into one of the chairs. He looked horrible as he turned toward Krem.

"Father, I know how you despise dishonesty, and I am sorry for lying to you. I have been seeing Aztrion for more than a year now.

We want to marry, and we are expecting a child. We have been meeting at my place in the mountains to be together by setting up fake captures of her by my most loyal men. We knew that no one would accept us being together. I rushed out so abruptly because I last left her at the mountain house two days ago, and she was supposed to go home, having once again escaped her captures. When I arrived at the mountain house, I found her injured and unable to even recognize me. She fell and hit her head against one of the gold trees where I found her. I brought her to Azmora's cottage straight away. Azmora said she has a concussion, is dehydrated, and needs rest. The baby seems fine as far as Azmora can tell. She said it was lucky she was found just in time." Kalem turned his attention to Alan. "I owe you a thanks for bringing news of her missing. I would have never found her in time had you not come. Thank you, Alan."

Alan nodded acknowledgment to Kalem. He felt uncomfortable taking credit for something that was chance on his part. Alan forgot Krem was even still sitting there; he had been quietly listening this whole time.

Finally, he spoke, "I am not pleased about you lying to me, Kalem. A house divided cannot stand. With that being said, I can understand why you had to sneak around. I have been a stubborn old man, holding grudges for far too long. It has taken some harsh, but true words from Alan to make me see this. We have come full circle. The love of my son's life and my grandchild were almost killed in a similar fashion as Rhea. I declare this minute to put an end to this senseless feud. Alan, would you be my emissary with the emperor so he doesn't think this a trick?"

"I will surely do what I can, but it may take more than me to convince him of this sudden change."

"I will be in my study preparing a correspondence for you to deliver to him, Alan. Krhea, please see that I am not disturbed until I am finished praying and writing. Also provide for our guest and see that he has a bed and whatever he may need until I send for him." Krem disappeared in a flourish of urgency from before their eyes.

Kalem said to no one in particular, "That was easier than I would have ever imagined."

"I am glad I am to be an aunt, but hurt that you kept this from me, Kalem," said Krhea.

He hung his head, more out of worry for Aztrion than embarrassment from his sister's comment.

"Would you follow me, Alan? It is getting late, and you must be tired."

Alan wished he had told Krem he would have to leave at sunrise, but would return shortly. Instead he explained to Krhea so she could tell her father when he emerged from his study.

He lay on the bed in the room Krhea provided and thought about all that transpired that day. This all seemed too good to be true. Part of him was saying to be cautious as he drifted off to sleep.

CHAPTER EIGHTEEN

Alan felt himself in a sickening dream of falling and spinning. He forced his eyes open in hopes of waking from the dream only to find himself in a spinning cell back on earth. He attempted to close his eyes again but was too late. He had to roll from his bunk to throw up in the toilet. When the world returned to normal, he brushed his teeth and washed up. Then he pulled his shank from his sock and hid it among the piles of legal work so the officers or property wouldn't find it. He checked his pocket and sure enough came out with a handful of wood chips. This was a very disappointing development.

Alan decided to make a coffee and sit down and write Grandma Rose a letter to encourage her and assure her he would be fine. When breakfast was brought around, the guard told Alan he would be moving to another tier at some point today. Alan tried to put up an argument to remain in this cell, but the guard said they had orders to shift six people around. Alan tried to convince the guard that a simple tier move wouldn't justify his stuff being sent to property. It was like talking to a wall though.

Alan moved, as he was given no choice. Two days later, he still had no property, so at breakfast time, he asked the guard if he would call property about his stuff.

"That is beyond my job description," he said.

"On Azcob's throne, I swear that it is important I get my personal property today," Alan said, pleading with the guard.

The prison guard's name was James Pike. He was average in height, but overweight as most of the prison guards were. Pike didn't like his life or his job, and in turn, tried to make the prisoners he was in charge of, as miserable as his limited authority would allow.

"You know the rules, Eliot. You'll get your stuff after the property officer goes through it and sends it down to us."

Then, with a look of wonder on his face, Pike said, "What was it you said a minute ago? You swear on whose throne?"

"Never mind," Alan said, shaking his head. He then began pacing his empty cell with the look of a man carrying a tremendous weight on his shoulders.

Pike walked away from Alan's cell, thinking, *These prisoners always act like they have some major appointment to keep.* He laughed a hateful laugh that echoed throughout the cellblock as he slammed the steel gate shut.

Alan stopped his pacing and started doing pushups to occupy his mind and expel some of the anxious energy he felt coursing through him. He then drifted off into thought of what brought him to this point in life. He was shaken from his thoughts sometime later by the guard tapping his keys on the bars of his cell.

"You want yard time, Eliot?"

"Yeah, give me a minute to throw my sneakers on."

"Hurry up, then I have a whole tier to put out."

Alan stepped up to the bars turning his back to the officer and putting his hands through the slot to be cuffed from behind.

"Cracking seventeen!" yelled the guard. He opened the cell door, and Alan stepped out. The officer took him by the arm, escorting him down the hall to the yard exit. As they reached the end of the hall, there were some boxes piled up along the wall. Alan saw his name written in black marker on one of the boxes. "Is that my property?" Alan asked the guard.

"I don't know. That stuff has been there for a couple days now since we did all the moves."

"Do you mean they never even sent our stuff to Property?"

"Sorry, Eliot, it's not my department. Putting you out for your exercise is my job."

As the guard brought the last inmate out to the exercise yard, Alan asked if he could see the sergeant of the unit.

"If he isn't busy, I will mention it to him after I have my coffee."

"Thanks, I really appreciate you giving me a minute of your time, Officer Belansky."

The guard looked oddly at Alan as he walked away. He probably wasn't used to having a civil conversation with an inmate in this setting.

Alan spent the hour walking the edges of the cage having passing conversations with the other inmates while keeping an eye out for the unit sergeant.

When the hour was up and the officers came to start bringing guys in, Officer Belansky said, "I'll take Eliot in first. Eliot, back up to be cuffed."

As they walked in, Alan asked if the officer had possibly spoken to the unit sergeant, but he didn't answer. As they got to his cell, the guard yelled out, "Cracking seventeen." He opened the cell and shoved Alan in, saying, "Get in your cell and don't give me any crap, Eliot!"

As Alan stumbled into the cell, he saw the box of property sitting on the bunk. He turned and looked at Officer Belansky. He smiled and put his finger in front of his lips to quiet Alan.

"Back up, so I can remove the cuffs."

Alan mouthed the words *thank you* silently. He had a newfound respect for this particular guard.

Alan waited until all the other inmates were in their cells, and the other guards were finished going up and down the tier before he unpacked his property. He didn't want to get Belansky in trouble with his fellow officers. The book was the first thing he dug out of the box and lovingly set it on the desk. Once he finally had everything situated in his cell, he lay back and gave some thought to how a kind word had made such a difference in this situation. He resolved to make a change in how he conducted himself within the prison. He hoped in some weird way that *his* proclamation of change would hold Krem to *his* similar proclamation to change. He would find out that night. He wished he could get some sleep to make the time go by faster, but he was so excited that wasn't going to happen.

He decided to make a list of ways he could change and what things he could do to facilitate his release from prison sooner. He whiled away the rest of the day doing this and that.

Finally, it was time to read Azterl's advice:

Entry 9

It appears you have made great headway, at least on the surface. The world you seek to save has a deep-seated history and is filled with passionate devotions. Don't be fooled into thinking change will come so easily. Change doesn't always fit into everyone's plans.

Luckily, you will see how a switch can benefit the most deserving of those in Azor. At the same time, great loss can bring about a new day of healing. Never underestimate the one-mindedness of an individual with long-standing hatred.

I wish you success. Keep your eyes open even for what is in plain sight. Good luck!

Alan sat the book on his chest and closed his eyes for a moment before invoking Azterl's spell. He wanted to be sure he was ready for whatever was facing him in Krem's castle upon his return. He would return to the bed he was asleep in when he left, so that wouldn't be a problem. His main concern was that he wouldn't have any protection against magic. Maybe he could try to convince Krhea to put a spell of protection on him. He would have to play it by ear.

"Well, here goes."

He covered his sneakers with the blanket, took the book off his chest, took a deep breath, and invoked Azterl's spell.

He wasn't sure if he was finally getting used to this, or it was just a lucky trip, but he was on the bed in the castle room in no time. He lay there a minute, then whispered Krhea's name. He hoped she was tuned into the castle as usual and would sense his presence. It literally took less than a minute for her to pop into the room, startling him.

"Krhea, you scare the heck out of me when you do that, but it's nice to see you."

"Thank you, Alan." She blushed. "Where have you been? It's been nearly a week since you left."

"I got caught up in my world. Believe me, it's not my fault. What have I missed? Is Aztrion okay?"

"Yes, she is much better. So much has happened, and you made it back just in time. Tonight is the big night."

"You'll have to tell me all about it, but first, can you do me a favor, Krhea?"

"What do you need, Alan?"

"Do you remember the spell you cast for me before, which protected me from other's magic being used against me? Could you do that again for me?"

"I can, but why would you need that, Alan?"

"I would just feel more comfortable, Krhea."

"*Kowto kwach, kulm*! There you go, Alan. But I am telling you, it's not necessary. Everyone is getting along. The big event tonight is a signing of a peace agreement between my father and Emperor Azcob."

"Well, why didn't you say so?"

"I tried, Alan. You're just like the other men in this castle. You only listen when you want."

Alan laughed.

"Father has been waiting for your return. We didn't think you were going to be back in time to attend the signing."

Alan silently thanked Officer Belansky in his head, but out loud said, "Yeah, I almost didn't make it."

"Come on, I'll take you to Father's study. He's working on last-minute plans."

They talked as they walked. It appeared that in his absence, Krem and Azcob had gotten together and made plans for a public signing of a peace agreement and wedding celebration joining Aztrion and Kalem. Everyone was meeting at Emperor Azcob's castle in Azkrem that evening.

When they arrived at Krem's study, Krhea knocked softly and called out, "Father, Alan has returned. Can we come in?"

The study door opened of its own volition, and Krem sitting at his desk said, "We didn't think you were coming back. That would have been unfortunate since you are a significant party in this new future of Azor."

Alan was struck by Krem's seemingly genuine joy about all this.

"Father, should I get drinks?"

"Thanks, sweetheart. Alan, have a seat while I finalize this treaty for tonight." He pointed toward the chair he had cleared for Alan just a week ago.

As Alan approached the chair, he stumbled over the pile of stuff Krem had thrown on the floor while clearing the chair. He reached down to straighten the pile some and was shocked to see three books in the pile. Sure enough, as he read the titles, one was *The Pilgrim's Progress*. He picked it up and asked Krem if he could look at it.

"Just be careful, Alan. That book is over six-hundred-Azor-years-old."

Alan did his best to contain his excitement as he sat down with the book cradled carefully in his lap.

"Krem, could I possibly ask a favor?"

"What do you need, Alan? I would say you have something coming for all you've done."

"Could you add a clause into your treaty stating that it's hereby illegal to hunt or harm azkibitz?"

"Why would you ask that? There aren't even any left as far as I can tell."

"I was helped by one on a couple different occasions, and I would like to repay the favor by helping to preserve the ones that still exist."

"Well, if I am going to truly move on, that is the least I could do. Let it be written, let it be law." He turned to add it to his writings, and Alan took the few minutes to open the book and flip through the pages. Nothing was obvious right off, but he figured Azterl wouldn't make the riddle easily recognized. Krem turned back toward him and said with a smile, "Your request is granted!"

Alan didn't know what to make of Krem. He seemed to have really done a three sixty.

"Now I would like to be alone for the morning if you don't mind. I will have Krhea escort you to the dining area when she returns. You can take the book if you like."

Just as he said this, Krhea showed up at the study door.

"Thanks for the drink, hon. Do you mind entertaining our guest until it's time to leave for Azkrem?"

"Not at all, Father."

"Thanks again for the favor, Krem," Alan said as he got up to leave with Krhea.

They walked to the dining area, and Alan asked, "How is everyone getting to Azkrem?"

"We will all go together. We will pool our magic and easily travel that distance as a group. Kalem is already there with Aztrion."

"Is Kasan here?"

"Yes, he will travel with us when Father says it is time to go."

"Will you be able to bring me along?"

"As I said, our combined strength will easily accommodate you, Alan. We wouldn't leave you behind."

"What about your spell? Will it prevent the combined magic traveling spell?"

"My spell protects you from others' magic, not mine. With the strength of a joint spell, my magic will easily carry you by itself. Don't worry, Alan. I could remove the spell if you wish."

"No, I would prefer to err on the side of caution if you don't mind."

"Whatever you prefer, Alan."

"Is it okay if I read a little while?"

"Actually, I have a ton of stuff to do before we go, so by all means, read to your heart's content."

Alan figured he would look at the book systematically to try to discern the riddles whereabouts. He checked out the cover, index, epilogue, and nothing seemed out of the ordinary. Next he decided to read the beginning of each chapter. He wasn't exactly sure what he was looking for, so he read the last few lines of the previous chapter and then the beginning of the new chapter to check for continuity. The first section had ten chapters with nothing he could see as odd. He started going through the second section, and at the beginning of chapter three, there was a story which didn't tie in with the previous chapter.

Alan read:

> A father of two young men was in the twilight of his life and wanted to leave his estate to one of his twin sons. Being an unorthodox individual, he told the young men they would race their azdwarks, and the owner of the slower azdwark would be heir apparent and take over the estate forthwith. The men both protested that the other would hold back his azdwark, so they would be slower and thus become the recipient of the estate. The father offered two words of advice to his sons. What were the two words?

Alan was positive this was Azterl's riddle since azdwarks would not be mentioned in *The Pilgrim's Progress*, that is for sure. He contemplated the riddle, but his thoughts were also distracted by who should receive Azterl's powers. He went one by one through the people he had met in Azor, listing pros and cons. No one really stood out above another, but there was definite no's on his list.

Alan decided to stop thinking so hard and try to think back on all Azterl's words, in the hopes there might be some direction in them. All of a sudden, the answer to the riddle and the recipient of the power hit him like a ton of bricks. He knew exactly what he had to do, but wasn't sure how it would suit the goals of Azor as a whole.

It was as if fate was confirming his decision because Krhea walked in, looking absolutely beautiful saying, "Father has summoned everyone. He wants to leave now for Azkrem. We are meeting on the tower roof in ten minutes. Would you help me gather a few things, Alan?"

"Why the sudden change of departure time?"

"You don't know Father. When he is ready to go, there's no stopping him."

Alan followed Krhea into a huge kitchen area where she had two large platters of food ready. They each carried one platter, down halls and up the stairs until Alan thought his arms would collapse. Krhea didn't seem bothered in the least.

"Alan, if you weren't carrying that book under your arm, that platter may be easier to carry."

"I promised Krem I would take care of it, and I am not finished with it just yet."

They reached the tower roof and saw Krem looking impatient as he stood waiting. Kasan was leaning against a club-ended staff made of gold, looking quite anxious to be on our way. Krhea apologized to Krem for being late. Then they all converged to within a foot of Alan and simultaneously shouted, "*Ketala!*"

Alan closed his eyes in anticipation of the spinning nausea that was to come. Instead, he instantly heard the sounds of a crowded hall. He opened his eyes and was shocked to see they were standing in a huge reception hall full of people. As the people closest to them realized who had just materialized in their midst, they became silent. The hush spread across the hall like wildfire as people turned and stared.

The voice of Emperor Azcob shouted so all could hear, "Welcome, Krem! We have been awaiting your arrival," as he made his way through the crowd toward them. Slowly, most of the people went back to their conversations.

CHAPTER NINETEEN

Alan found himself wandering around the hall, hoping for a chance to run into Azonia. There were so many people milling around, and there was still a couple of hours till the wedding and treaty signing would take place. Things seemed to be going amazingly, and this bothered him in a nagging way. He wasn't necessarily a pessimist. It was just that Azterl's words of warning kept ringing in his ears. It was so crowded in the hall and got worse as the event time drew closer. Alan figured that he might have a better chance of seeing Azonia as she came in since he didn't see her anywhere, so he went in the hall. He made his way to the front doors and felt an immediate relief as he stepped out onto the drawbridge and crossed the street into fresh air. The street was a bustle of activity in its own right but seemed quiet compared to the hall.

Alan wandered from shop to shop, intrigued by the different crafts for sale. Everyone seemed happy and celebrating in some fashion. He guessed that the people must have looked at this like an Independence Day of sorts. He stopped and watched a group of children gathering together down the street by an alleyway. They were excited and shouting loudly to one another as they pointed down the alley. When they began joining together in a fashion of blocking the alley, Alan decided to investigate further himself, in case they were bullying some unfortunate kid. As he drew closer, he was convinced they were up to no good as he saw a couple of kids throw small rocks into the alley. As Alan came to the edge of the building, he could see clearly into the alley over their heads. There was an azkibitz in the farthest part of the alley attempting to stay out of range of the projectiles thrown by the kids. Alan yelled and started waving his arms like a madman and slapping his hand against the book he carried. The children were so taken aback by this giant with blond hair that they scattered in all directions screaming like they'd seen the Boogie Man himself. Alan watched them run away and laughed just as he was knocked off his feet. It was Lucky, and he was so happy to see Alan he knocked him on his butt in the street. Alan was equally happy to see Lucky and reached out while sitting in the dirt of the street and hugged Lucky to him.

"This is great, Lucky. You needed to be here today. You won't believe what I convinced Krem to do. He is going to—Hold on a minute, let me do this first."

Alan got up, brushed himself off, picked up the book he had dropped when Lucky knocked him over, and he heard a voice said, "Switch azdwarks, Alan Eliot!"

He hoped he had done it right, but nothing happened. Maybe the answer to the riddle wasn't right after all. He was so sure he had figured it out. Just as he was going to repeat himself, he felt and heard a deep, deep voice, saying, "You did good, Alan. You are the recipient of my powers."

Alan wondered if Lucky could hear the voice as well, but Lucky just sat there, looking at Alan to tell him about Krem.

"He can't hear me," the deep, deep voice said.

Alan startled a little from the realization that the voice had read his thoughts. He hadn't known what to expect, but this wasn't it.

He thought, *How do I cast a spell?*

"Just think about it, and I will help you."

Alan thought about what he had made his mind up to do while at Krem's castle.

A couple of seconds went by, and then the deep, deep voice said, "That is a noble desire, but it is also something that will most likely take *all* the power to accomplish. You will be left with no magic. Are you sure this is your decision?"

Alan didn't hesitate even a second and out loud said, "Yes, this is what I desire most."

Lucky was looking at Alan, thinking, *What is wrong with you, Alan? Are you going crazy?*

Both he and Alan were shocked that those words came out of Lucky's mouth. Lucky stood, and to his amazement, stood fully erect.

"This is impossible. I am not on the mountain and how am I able to talk?"

Alan started laughing uncontrollably and couldn't answer. Each time he tried to talk, the look on Lucky's face caused him to bust out in laughter even harder.

Lucky kicked Alan hard in the shin. It succeeded for the most part in helping Alan get back under control.

"I am sorry, Azdebar. I was just so pleased to see you again in your rightful state that I lost control."

"What has happened, Alan? What did you do?"

"Slow down, Azdebar. I cast a spell that enables your people to no longer be restricted to the mountain in order to stand and speak."

"Are you crazy? You have doomed my people! What were you thinking? I must leave for the mountain right away."

"No, Azdebar. I was telling you that Krem is signing into law today a decree stating it is illegal to hunt or harm any azkibitz from this day forth."

"And you believed him? After they tried to exterminate my race? How could you do this?"

"Luck—I mean, Azdebar, I wouldn't put you or your family into danger. This is going to happen. I will see to it. I give you my promise."

"It has been done now, so I pray you are right. Tell me how this all came about."

They walked together back toward the hall, and Alan explained the important points of what had taken place since their capture that night so long ago. As they arrived outside the hall, they ran into Azire. He was walking with a young lady holding onto his arm, which Alan assumed was his sister.

"Hey, Azire, great to see you," said Alan while waving him over to where he and Azdebar stood.

"Boy, when you go on a mission, you don't mess around, Azearth," Azire said.

The men shook hands and clapped each other on the back heartily. Then they turned to their companions, and Alan introduced Azdebar.

"Great to finally meet you. We have heard about your exploits of courage in aiding Azearth. I would like to introduce my fiancé and the love of my life—Azrean."

Alan nearly passed out. "I thought you and—I'm sorry, Azrean. It is my great pleasure to meet you."

Alan gave Azire a quizzical look and said, "Azire, can I get a minute privately before the ceremony begins?"

The two of them walked a few feet away, and Alan whispered, "I thought you and Azonia were together?"

Azire laughed a deep barrel laugh and said, "That's why you act weird when she's around? No, Azearth. We are like brother and sister, and I swore an oath to always be in her service to make sure no harm comes to her. She is actually attracted to you but feels that you aren't interested." Azire laughed again, slapping Alan on his back. "Let's go get a seat for the festivities, my friend."

People were beginning to take their seats on each side of the hall, and Alan could see Emperor Azcob, the empress, and Krem involved in a conversation on the dais. Krhea stood a few feet away talking to Azonia. She was more beautiful at that moment than ever before to Alan.

Azire led them down the aisle to seats on the right side about twenty feet from the dais. Alan took the seat closest to the aisle. He noticed people stretching their necks trying to see Azdebar, and he was eating up the attention, standing straight and proud. Seeing him like this assured Alan that he had made the right decision regardless of the cost. He tried numerous times while sitting there to reach out to Azterl's voice in his head, but there was no response. The spell obviously depleted all the power in accomplishing the task.

Alan watched Azonia brush her hair back from her face and thought she glanced his way for just a second. He thought everyone in the hall must hear his heart beating.

Emperor Azcob raised his arm, and a hush slowly took the room over.

"Good citizens of Azor, if everyone could take their places, we are about to get underway. On this momentous occasion, we celebrate a declaration of peace and a joining of families. There is no day in the history of Azor as important as today. So please stand for the reading of the treaty by the illustrious Wizard Krem."

People clapped, stomped, hooted, and hollered with uncontrollable joy until Azcob raised his arm once again. As Krem read the treaty he had so eloquently written, there wasn't a dry eye in the house. When he decreed the azkibitz as protected citizens of Azor, Azdebar had to hold onto the back of the seat in front of him to remain standing.

All of a sudden, an angry shout came from the rear of the hall, "*Kiev khar toum!*" Everyone who was turning to look back was frozen in midmovement. As Alan glanced with his eyes, he realized everyone in the hall was frozen in place except for him and Kasan. He watched without moving as Kasan walked down the aisle with his club-ended gold staff.

"Listen to me, old man. Your time has passed. This showing of weakness will ruin us!" Kasan yelled for all to hear.

Alan pretended to be frozen like everyone else. He knew it was Krhea's protection spell making him the only one in the room unaffected by Kasan's immobilization spell.

Kasan continued up the aisle, shouting, "I'll crush your head under my scepter, Azcob, and all of Azterl's family, one by one."

As he walked past Alan, he pointed his staff at Azire and said, "I'll be right back for you and that filthy azkibitz."

Alan waited for him to pass and then made his move. He hit Kasan on the back of his neck with both hands in a sledgehammer motion, causing him to crumple to the ground like a wet rag.

Alan knew the spell wouldn't be broken by Kasan being knocked unconscious. He desperately tried to reach out to the deep, deep voice of Azterl with his mind, but there was only silence. He would have to solve this through brute force as before with Kasan.

Alan positioned himself behind Kasan, holding him in a choke hold without applying pressure until he felt him returning to consciousness. He applied just enough pressure to assure that Kasan took him seriously.

"Well, here we are again, Kasan. I guess you haven't learned your lesson that I am the strongest of wizards here. You will never stand a chance of destroying or enslaving Azor. Now, as much as I would like to end you, which would surely break your spell. I will give you the chance to reverse your spell immediately."

Kasan slumped in defeat and said, "*Kepate keline!*"

There was an immediate commotion as the spell released everyone at once. They all saw and heard what took place while under the immobilization spell. The people now started to panic and rush out of their seats.

Krem shouted, "*Kehan khalm!*" and the room instantly became quiet. "I apologize for casting a spell on all of you, but I felt it necessary to bring about order. The spell was a simple one of calming, which I will remove in a moment. This sad turn of events by my son is *my* fault. He lived with my revengefulness and anger for so long he knows nothing else. I give you my word you are all safe, and this occasion is long overdue. Please remain calm and join us in completing this celebration when I remove the calming spell. He waited a second for his words to sink in, then shouted, "*Khalm kehano!*"

The people calmly headed back to their seats. Krem came down the aisle toward Alan and Kasan, and Kasan started to speak, "Father, I—"

Krem waved his hand and said, "*Kiev khar toum! Ketala!*" Both Krem and Kasan disappeared from the hall.

As Alan got back to his feet, the hall erupted in clapping and yelling directed at him. He looked up on the dais to find Azonia, and she was excitedly clapping and smiling. She waved her arm to get him to come up with her just as Krem popped back onto the dais. Everyone quieted down, expecting there to be an announcement by him about Kasan. Alan was sure that Kasan was residing in the special room back at Krem's castle.

Krem just turned to Azcob and said, "Shall we continue?"

Emperor Azcob turned to Aztrion and Kalem, saying, "Marriage first or signing?"

They turned to each other and, without a word, nodded to the other before Kalem said, "We would like to marry under the new Azor treaty, so—signing first."

Everyone laughed while Krem and Azcob moved into position to sign the treaty. Azonia smiled at Alan since he was stuck at his seat now until the celebration was completed. His heart soared in his chest with happiness.

Wizard Krem and Emperor Azcob leaned over and signed the treaty simultaneously. As they raised up from the signing, the room erupted in applause, and Alan felt himself falling through the nothingness, spinning round and round. When the spinning stopped, he opened his eyes to find himself in his cell on earth.

Over the next few days, Alan tried to invoke Azterl's spell, but there were no new entries, and nothing happened. He assumed that, at the signing of the treaty, the spell on Azterl's book was completed. Azor was no longer under attack. Alan's heart was crushed over losing Azonia but glad that the people of Azor were safe, and Lucky's family was free.

A couple of weeks passed with no change, and Alan resolved himself to be thankful for what he had here. His grandma Rose needed him as much as he needed her.

Just while he was thinking about her, Officer Pike walked by and threw his mail across the cell at him. Alan instantly saw red and yelled, "Hey, Pike, you are a—"

At that instant, Alan heard and felt a deep, deep voice from within say, "Alan, remember your commitment to change."

ABOUT THE AUTHOR

Mr. Talbot is fifty-five years old. He resides in Gardner, Massachusetts. He is committed to change his life and those around him. He facilitates Toastmasters, alternatives to violence, and many other positive self-help workshops.

He is a musician, and his music can be found on Amazon, Spotify, iTunes, etc. under the name Razor Wire Rhythms, as well as D. Alan Talbot.

CPSIA information can be obtained
at www.ICGtesting.com
Printed in the USA
LVHW052035250820
664152LV00011B/285